The Botanical Witches and the Vicereina's Foulard

The Botanical Witches and the Vicereine´s Foulard

J.M. Alkonada

Published by j.m. alkonada, 2024.

While every precaution has been taken in the preparation of this book, the publisher assumes no responsibility for errors or omissions, or for damages resulting from the use of the information contained herein.

THE BOTANICAL WITCHES AND THE VICEREINE´S FOULARD

First edition. August 11, 2024.

ISBN: 979-8224450152

Written by J.M. Alkonada.

Table of Contents

chapter 1
The Perfumed Policeman

Barcelona, in 1967 at the Police Headquarters, Inspector Simón Borrull, a reserved twenty-eight-year-old man, a good professional (although not too professional), integrated into the police force, felt that he had another hidden vocation for which one day he would be called.

Perfectly dressed, properly combed but without gel in his hair as was the custom among his companions and above all happily perfumed. In his pockets he had a flask of perfume, a deck of tarot cards and a gun.

That morning he was sitting in his office, looking engrossed at old photographs of his family: his parents and grandparents, he thought that his family was nothing like the other people he knew. How was it possible that he only had fragments of memories of everyone? Are they fragments of happy moments at Christmas and some birthdays where the entire family got together? Everyone except his mysterious grandmother Angelica, of whom he had heard so much but did not remember her face, perhaps it was possible that he had never seen her, although as a child in his imagination he remembered her as the superheroine "Wonder Woman" from the comics that he she devoured before going to sleep, she remembered her grandfather Felix's emotion when he spoke to her about her and the adventures they lived together, under the attentive

inquisitive gaze of her mother who did not want those topics to be mentioned, much less the word witch. In At that moment, a sudden interruption caused by police officer Albert Cusidó overthrew his train of thought.

"Mr. Inspector has informed us of another attack on a perfume establishment," said police officer Albert Cusidó.

-Another one! Three in a week, well let's go to the police car and make sure you take the keys - Inspector Simón Borrull joked -

When the inspector and his assistant arrived at the perfume sales establishment on Canuda Street, they were surprised because that robbery or robbery was different from the previous ones. Inside the establishment, a pitched battle had taken place. The two girl shop assistants defended themselves from their attackers. Despite being badly injured, the criminals were on the ground with bloody faces and could barely be aware of the beating they had received. The ambulances arrived and took the injured to the hospital, guarded by the police. Inspector, shall we return to the police station?

–No Albert! I want to investigate what has happened here. How is it possible that two girls who barely weigh forty-five kilos have been able to face four men as big as towers and also the money box is intact like in the previous

attacks on other perfume stores? What would they be looking for?

-Who knows? Maybe they are those long-haired bands that listen to rock music – said agent Cusido.

– These guys are criminals hired by someone.

The two police officers commented while looking at shelves full of perfumes and essential oils. Shortly after, Agent Albert found a bottle of perfume that aroused his curiosity...

–Mr. Inspector, can I keep this beautiful perfume, will I give it to my girlfriend?

Inspector Borrull looked at his assistant to see what he wanted to show him and when he saw that container an avalanche of memories flooded his mind, he soon remembered that his grandfather, Chief Commissioner Felix Borrull, years before he died, told him that there was a secret organization called " the Perfumed Society" which was thousands of years old and was composed of female botanists who were experts in perfumes of destiny and which was especially helped in solving many cases by two of them. Angelica, her grandmother and

Severina were called princesses and witches. His mother did not like these stories but he was curious, although he also

suspected that all this could be a story for girls. But my grandfather's words resonated in my head...

–Yes Simón, I was like you, for me all those things were old wives' tales, but they saved my life and if you become a police officer like me, it is possible that they will save yours in the future. Their coat of arms was a perfume bottle in the shape of a woman with angel wings, don't forget. That was the perfume that agent Albert Cusidó held in his hand.

–Inspector, is something wrong with you? It's frozen still!

–Give me that perfume! We will begin to investigate, starting with this test, it surely has a meaning, it reminds me of something. Now let's return to the headquarters, we have to start a line of investigation that will be totally different.

They got into the police car and shortly after they arrived at the police station on Trafalgar Street when the car stopped and they entered the police station, a riot of voices and complaints from a large group of men and women who were arguing with the officers. of cop...

"Silence, everyone shut up, Officer on duty, what is happening here?" asked Inspector Borrull.

–Some police officers have discovered some suspicious activities in a premises near the port and they have carried out a raid and here we have them –said the officer on duty

–Everyone calm down, you red-haired girl! What's it called? Inspector Borrull questioned.

My name is Carmen Vidal, and we were not doing anything illegal. We wanted to organize an Astrology Congress

–You mean astronomy! Are you students

–No, I said astrology correctly and we are not university students, we are dedicated to investigating the movements of the zodiac in the cosmos.

–Damn what a day I have today! Agent Cusido, go to my office and bring me the manual on suspicious activities and other associations.

-Yes sir..

After a few minutes, the manual was handed over to Inspector Borrull, he opened it and ran his index finger over all the pages. There were indications prohibiting political meetings, union associations and Jewish Masonic collusion, but nothing that talked about astrology, all while he was surrounded by All the others present, some even

put their heads into the manual and as that situation began to bother him, he closed the little book.

–Well, gentlemen, it does not say here that what you are doing is illegal, so you can all leave. And now I'm going to my office. Albert come with me! –the inspector stated emphatically.

When the inspector pushed the door of his office he noticed that in his jacket pocket there was a note with a drawing, how strange he thought this note is not mine, when he looked at it carefully he observed that it had the same drawing as the bottle of perfume that he had Found Agent Cusido, he ran out of his office down the stairs to the exit door of the police headquarters in the hope of meeting the astrological group, but everyone had disappeared through the numerous streets of the Gothic, after a while Agent Albert appeared, who ran after him.

–Mr. Inspector uff. Is something wrong? What did you see?

–They left this note in my pocket, it has a drawing that is the logo of the "Perfumed Society", an organization that my family has told me so much about, it is sure that it is a message for me.

–And that organization is legal!

–It was in the past! Now almost nothing is legal, let's go back to my office I want to review the documents I have from this organization

Once sitting in his office chair and with the folder of documentation in his hands about the "Perfumed Society" he reviewed everything written about the organization and found nothing different from everything his grandfather had told him about it, he could tell yourself that you knew it by heart; the confrontation with the woman called Black Lady, the explosions, the shootings in the street and premises, the dead police officers, the children kidnapped for a bloody ritual, everything that could be written in a police report, clearly omitting

There is the secret and magical part that could not be recorded in any file, referring to fragrances of immortality, perfumes and miraculous cosmetics where very influential people from the city and the rest of the country paid enormous amounts of money, and that charges were never filed against To round out the story there was also an ancient angel called "the beautiful light" who granted eternal youth through an emerald, and all this sixty years ago.

For Inspector Simón Borrull, the adventure that his grandfather Felix told him when he was a child baffled him. On the one hand, it seemed like the fantasy of an

older man, but he also remembered how his face lit up when he spoke to him about grandmother Angelica and her

friend Severina. two incredible Botanical Witches wrapped in an aura of mystery and secrecy.

He again took the note that was left in his pocket and compared the drawing he had with the bottle of perfume that his assistant gave him and it was the same logo of the "Perfumed Society" at the bottom of the note he saw that he had written down an address it was about. from a residence for the elderly on a street in the best area of Barcelona, his name was Father Berenguer.

"Albert, we're leaving right now, take this note, get a police car and we'll go to this address," Inspector Simon ordered.

After twenty minutes of traveling by car through the streets of Barcelona, they arrived at the place indicated in the note and once they had parked the car a few meters from the residence, they walked next to the entrance door once they rang the bell a few minutes later it opened. A middle-aged woman in a nurse's uniform came to the door.

-Good morning madam, I am a police inspector, could I speak with
the director of this center.
-Director! Sure, come in. Do you have an appointment? If not, wait in
the hallway – the nurse commented.

The inspector and his assistant Albert sat on two comfortable sofas
while their gaze took in everything around them. The furniture and
tapestries of exquisite taste
were in accordance with what they expected to see, given the area
where the residence was located. A short time later, the lady appeared
and opened the door for them, indicating that they should follow her.
They walked down a long hallway until they reached the door of an
office where the person in charge of the center was waiting.
–Good morning gentlemen, I am the director Elena Berenguer.
–Good morning madam, I am Inspector Simón Borrull and this is my
assistant, Agent Albert Cusidó.
The reason for my visit is for a line of investigation, we have a card with
a drawing of a perfume logo and underneath is written the address and
name of this residence as you can see. Does this relationship tell you
anything?
–Well no, I don't understand why there is a card printed with a drawing
of a perfume and our name from the Berenguer center, I haven't given
permission for something like that.
–I understand, tell me your last name is Berenguer as the name of the
residence.
– Yes, this center was inaugurated by my uncle Father Berenguer with a
financial contribution from the church.
–I will explain the reason for my visit, a few days ago in the city there
were a series of attacks on some perfume shops perpetrated by very
professional and violent people, this morning I found this bottle of
perfume and this card with the same drawing and this address.

–I don't know what to tell you, there are only elderly people here and I don't think that between breakfast and lunch they'll do perfume shops. They barely stay awake, I don't know how I can help you inspector.

–Could you provide me with a list of all the residents and workers of the center.

-Yes of course.

The director got up from her seat and went to a small filing cabinet that was located near the window that illuminated her office, extracted a folder from one of her drawers and handed it to the inspector.

–Thank you, let's see what we find.

He reviewed all the names that were written down on the list that the director provided him and he was not sure what he could find that would help him in the investigation, until

he saw one that took him back to his childhood when his grandfather told him about his police adventures.

–Inspector! Have you found anything?–Agent Cusido inquired.

–This person Crisol Portabella! Where is he? I want to talk to her.

–Inmate Crisol, who recently came to this center and is the one in the best state of health, but she is far from being a criminal, she is eighty-six years old although she looks less than that, to tell the truth.

–Yes, I know, I met her when I was a child, she was a friend of my grandfather, she worked as a taxidermist and perfumer.

–My God! How can it be both things... Anyway, I'll take him to the pavilion where he is.

They walked down a long corridor with the director Elena Berenguer in front where they arrived at a pavilion, where there were numerous elderly people, who were carrying out numerous re-educational activities such as educational games sitting around a table, some were reading books, and others were limited. to look out the large windows that overlooked an outside garden, one of those people was Crisol.

–Inspector there he is! It's the one in the corner looking out the window.

–Thank you ma'am, now if we excuse ourselves we will go say hello and chat with her.

–Well, if you need me I'll be in my office.

Simón and Albert, the two police officers, approached the woman who was sitting in a rocking chair, staring abstractedly at an indeterminate place on the street.

–Mrs. Portabella, I am Simón, the grandson of Commissioner Félix Borrull, you and my grandfather were friends when they were young, remember?

–The woman turned her head towards him and looked at him for a long, silent minute, until she finally smiled.

–Ahh, yes, you are little Simón, your grandfather took you by the hand when you were a child, together we would go out for walks through the streets and talk about old times. I remember that you liked cream tarts in exchange for your silence because sometimes Your mother didn't like me.

–Yes, I remember it very well, eighteen years have passed and I see that you feel very well. What is a Botanical Witch of her prestige doing in a nursing home?

The Cusido agent opened his mouth in amazement. It was the first time he had seen Inspector Borrull call an old woman a witch. Crisol looked at both police officers with fixedness and strength. The inspector knew that look. His grandfather had told him about it. It was the consequence of a clumsiness and indiscretion committed on his part.

–Ah, no, no, ha, ha, ha, that's an affectionate name that I used to say when I was a child to Mrs. Portabella. Cusido agent, go to the cafeteria and eat something in half an hour, I'll meet you.

-Yes sir!

When the agent was walking away towards the bar, Mrs. Crisol indicated with her hand that he should take a seat in a chair next to her.

–Well Simón, what is the reason for your visit? Crisol asked, now with an authoritative voice.

–This morning at the police headquarters someone left me this note in my jacket pocket. It has the logo of the "Perfumed Society."
and it has this address, and this place is nothing like what they told me when I was a child, so by the way, only you
are left, Mrs. Portabella, do you still belong to the "Society"?
–Please, Inspector Borrull, you know very well that these organizations are not currently allowed.
–Of course, of course, my grandfather told me that witches were very evasive and that it was difficult for him to understand and deal with them, but I promise to keep an open mind if you would like to communicate something important to me.
–Well Simón, let's talk about those perfume shops that have been attacked by men hired by someone, what are they looking for? Money, smell good, cosmetics for your girlfriends?
–I don't know, you tell me.
–Call me Crisol, because of the name, very well, as I said, these guys are looking for something very specific, a very special perfume that grants eternal youth or perhaps another power.
–Please Crisol, I'm not a child anymore. Also, as I remember, it was an angel's emerald and not a perfume that allows you to live hundreds of years, like the famous Black Lady I think I remember.
–Well, Simón, I see that you keep the memories of the family, well, well, and tell me how you explain that Commissioner Borrull in the year 1908 was shot three times, fell from a height of four stories and two days later he was discharged from the hospital. hospital. I was there that night and your grandfather was dying when he entered the ambulance accompanied by the botanical witches Angelica and Severina, I could see how they made him inhale a perfume and poured it on his wounds. The crucible explanation did not come to him again, he knew the story, but he never gave it much importance because he spent the summers on the beach with his parents and grandfather and he never saw any trace of any wound on his body.

–I know very well what you are thinking, Simón, there was no scar on his body, right? Well, let's continue at that time, police officer Lucas Sorní, your grandfather Felix's assistant, and I became boyfriends; he belonged to Commissioner Borrull's police brigade. and after a few years of working together as a forensic taxidermist in a dirty basement of the Trafalgar central police station, we went to America, specifically to California, we had a daughter. At that time there was a global fever for cinema, those films made millions of people dream. Thanks to my new knowledge about magical perfumes I was able to enter the movie mecca, Hollywood! Nothing less! crazy parties, full-throttle fun, luxury, lovers, French champagne, and more lovers, that was crazy, I remember the actor Rudolph Valentino, he was a very fun man, I laughed a lot with him, I gave him love filters, which made him He drove women crazy and because he also had one eye that stared at you and the other eye looked at the Pacific Ocean.

–Because he tells me all that! Melting pot

–Because that madness almost ended me, my health was ruined and my boyfriend Lucas had stopped seeing him for a long time, I barely had any news, only that he made some friends that were not recommended, I for my part tried to regain the balance of Bruja for something I had had formidable teachers like the members of the Perfumed Society when I lived in Barcelona, but one day I had an attack of coughing and cold sweat, I caught yellow fever, and at that moment, lying on the floor, I had a revelation about myself. My passion, the lack of control of my life, my taste for those things that make a woman lose herself, was that I, Crisol Portabella" was a crazy witch of the forest, my family called The Zero Arcanum were uncontrolled witches, and to make matters worse The situation: I invested all my money earned from the sale of amorous perfumes in the New York Stock Exchange and one Monday in 1929 the stock market collapsed and I lost everything. I had to flee because I owed money to some well-dressed Italians. And when I felt better I hid in an opium den, another bad decision for someone like me, that place didn't suit me, anyway I asked my ex Lucas Sorni for help, and after a few weeks, I will always remember seeing him appear among the people who were lying on the ground making their way until they reached me, were my

two dear witches and friends Severina and Angelica leaned towards me they looked at me intently and my friend the look of a witch makes your whole body vibrate! It was them ! And the most amazing thing of all was that they had the same face as twenty years ago, how was it possible! I hadn't even scratched their faces for a single minute, at first I thought it was the effect of opium, but that day I hadn't smoked, I was just resting, believe me! They had not aged.

–Excuse me Crisol, I have to go to the bathroom.

–Of course, of course I won't move from here.

Suddenly, the inspector stood up from his chair, looking displeased. He walked briskly to the end of the hallway and closed the bathroom door behind him. Sitting on the toilet bowl, he took out a flask from his jacket and put it in his mouth. He needed a drink. drink of liquor from his harvest, for years he had been trying to make his way as a botanical perfumer and now after hearing the story of Crisol he still wanted it much more. In his house he had a great variety of plants and flowers in a backyard but he couldn't make a miserable perfume, all of them spoiled, he introduced alcohol as a preservative in his mixtures, but it didn't work either, the aroma evaporated immediately and the energetic component did not appear. and finally he ended up drinking it as a herbal liquor, which became a drinking addiction and a problem. "Loving perfumes" and the worst thing was the laughter of his colleagues at the

police headquarters because of the smell. a "strange" not to mention a faggot who gave off his perfumes, which is why he didn't have any friends and was called "the perfumed one."

–Well, it's time to go back to Crisol.

He closed the door behind him and headed to meet his interlocutor.

–Well, Mrs. Portabella, you said that you saw your friends from your youth again and....

"Wow, wow, Simón, don't tell me that you drink perfumes," Crisol laughed loudly.

-How is it possible!

The inspector put his hand to his mouth and then to his nose, to see if his breath had given him away.

–Don't worry, Simón, I was a Botanical Witch, let's see by the smell, mint, sage, lavender, some rose petals and peppermint and forty-degree alcohol. Am I wrong? Come on, pass me the flask, I need a drink. But don't worry, I was a painful witch making perfumes, it was a disaster and since you finally drank it, well over time I learned and specialized in love filters.

–He told me that he saw his friends again...

–Ah yes, yes, they had not aged at all after twenty years. Incredible! Right? Fortunately, they came to my aid, they took me out of that den and took me to a luxurious hotel where we stayed for a week, there they took care of me, the botanical witches protected each other, we picked up my daughter from boarding school and We returned to Spain, specifically to Barcelona, for my part I entered the perfumed society again, of my dear witch friends I never saw them again and I imagine why, they had children Angelica with your grandfather and Severina with the Chinese Wei of astral travel.

–She said she knew why her savior friends disappeared.

–Imagine that one day you get out of bed and realize that your mother is younger than you, considering that children do not follow in their parents' footsteps, that fact would be a serious family disorder.

–You say that children do not follow in the footsteps of their parents. Why?

–Children are usually proud, they want to make their own way and having a witch mother is not usually part of their plans, but grandchildren are something else, they

I love having grandparents, the more mysterious and extravagant the better.

Inspector Borrull nodded his head, he remembered that when he visited his grandfather and had conversations about botanical witches he had to keep it a secret from the ears of his parents, especially from his mother who detested witchcraft and witchcraft.

–Good Good Crisol I confess that I liked the talk about her past but I know very well that botanical witches are not very given to telling little stories about their lives. You made me come for something else, right?

– That's right Simón, if you want to move forward in the case of the attacked perfumeries you will have to go look for my granddaughter, her name is Estela. I haven't seen her for about fourteen years. Now she must be about twenty-five years old. The last thing I know about her is that she tries to being a botanical witch and she has ended up being a silly witch, she has gotten into the hippie movement and believes in free and universal love, ha-ha-ha she is so naive.. The world we live in is always at war. Well , is in Ibiza in a commune dancing in a meadow with flowers in her hair and half naked. Here you have a photo of her.

–Crisol looks a lot like you.

–Yes, much more than you think, inspector.

–I don't see how a hippie girl can help me solve this case.

–I think so, look Simon, your arcana in the Tarot card is the Moon, you are pure intuition, you try to be creative because you remember the past in your unconscious dreams, but your duality confuses you, in the drawing of the card there are two towers, two plants, two dogs that bark at the moon, and a crab submerged in water that represents your hidden personality, it is very possible that your current police profession is not compatible with your desires but that is your destiny card. perfume contains clary sage oil, labdanum rockrose and damask rose and selacia mushroom juice. Simon, this fragrance will help you hear your inner voice, and choose your path.

Crisol placed a bottle of perfume in the inspector's hand who in turn brought it to his nose and inhaled it. He thought most of the time that he tried to make that fragrance that corresponded to his birth date and he never succeeded.

–Thank you, I tried many times, but it never worked out. You knew I would come to visit you, right?

–Carry it with you, it will always fill you with energy and self-confidence as long as you don't drink it, and as for your previous question, you have to join my granddaughter

who is also a botanical witch, she is the imagination and fantasy of a witch of the forest and who we usually call "The crazy one of the house" there is another person who will join you, you will discover it in due time... There have to be three of you, and form a magical triangle, only then will you be successful in your adventure.

–Well here comes my assistant, thank you very much Mrs. Crisol for everything, I will look for your granddaughter and we will see what happens.

They shook hands goodbye and once on the street they got into the car.

–Mr. Inspector, where are we going now?

–Cusido agent, you will visit the director of the clinical hospital and ask him for a report on a patient named Félix Borrull who was admitted with gunshot wounds in the summer of 1908. Now take me to the police headquarters..

–Felix Borrull? Is he a relative of yours, nineteen hundred and eight?

–If it was my grandfather...

When they both left the perimeter of the residence driving along the main road, a car tried to hit him and throw them into the ditch. The inspector took out his gun, but a second

side impact from the other vehicle caused him to drop the gun on the floor of the car. The carelessness was providential because a shot that was intended for him when he was bending down to pick up the weapon hit Agent Cusido in the shoulder, causing the police vehicle to stop. The other attacking car stopped about thirty meters ahead and several men got out. of the vehicle pointing their weapons, while Inspector Borrull took agent Albert Cusidó out of the car and laid him on the ground protected by the front of the car while he repelled the attack by shooting again and again.

–Agent, how are you, okay? Avoid fainting.

–Sir, have my weapon, I can't use it.

Inspector Borrull knew that he had to hit the shot and take advantage of the ammunition otherwise they would be lost, those guys knew what they were doing without a doubt they were professional criminals, suddenly the sound of a motorcycle that jumped over the attackers and skidded into a meter of them made everyone stop shooting and with an acrobatic jump one

The unknown girl began to deliver a large number of blows with fists and legs in the air and in the face of the assailants, causing them to return to the car and flee.

–You've seen that, sir, I've never seen anyone fight like that, much less a girl.

But police officer Simón Borrull was not at all strange, his grandfather in one of his battles told him how his partner Angelica fought, she was capable of taking down several men in a matter of minutes in a very similar way to that stranger, who at that moment was approached the two of them. She was a thin, six-foot-six, brunette girl with slanted eyes but not completely Asian, twenty-six years old, dressed in a black leather skirt and a biker jacket, walking with a firm step, to the inspector she seemed like someone with character.

–Thank you very much for your help, Miss?

–Sevange, our families know each other, Mr. Borrull, and if you do a deduction exercise you will guess who I am. Now we have to take your partner to the hospital.

–Yes, of course, and I repeat, thank you very much.

The inspector helped agent Albert Cusidó get into the car and they drove to the hospital followed by Sevange's motorcycle. About half an hour they arrived at the medical center and entered through the emergency door and some nurses took care of the injured police officer.

–He has a gunshot wound to the shoulder.

"Very well, we'll take care of it. If you want, you can wait in the room at the end of the hallway," the nurses hurried to say.

–Well, thank you, we'll be there.

Simón and Sevange walked towards the waiting room and once inside they sat opposite each other.

–Come inspector ask.

–No, you told me to do a deduction exercise, right? Do you know my name, our families know each other, he told me, you fight very well, karate?

–Kung fu, a martial art

-OK. You have slanted eyes, and green, so you can only be related to Wei-lin and the Botanical Witch Severina.

–I see that you are aware of our family secret. My name is Sevange wei Visconti de Saint Germain, Severina's granddaughter. and you are Angelica's grandson, we have to work together to resolve a painful matter. Do you have any idea who they are attacking us and what they are looking for?

–No, I don't know, we are investigating who is behind this. Do you have anything to do with some of the affected

establishments? Wait, it was you who knocked out those thugs in the perfume store!

–If it was me, they beat my employees, luckily I was in the back room making perfumes when the assault occurred, I had to break some heads and shortly after I called the police and an ambulance later I left through a hidden back door, like You know, witches always have a secret exit.

I think those guys are looking for us, I followed you when you visited a nursing home, where our beloved Crisol is, you already know the rest. Now it's your turn, Simon.

–A series of circumstances led me to the residence where I had a talk with Crisol Portabella, a mythical witch. She told me that we had to find her granddaughter Estela, a young botanical witch turned hippie in Ibiza, and form a magical triangle, I don't know how. Explain this to my superiors when they ask me for a report.

–Well, Simon, something will occur to you, now I'm going home. We'll see each other tomorrow at noon at the airport. We'll go look for Estela, goodbye.

Inspector Borrull watched as that mysterious girl walked away, it was strange, their families were inseparable, their two grandmothers Severina and Angelica disappeared together traveling the world in search of perfumes of power and yet Sevange, Estela and himself did not know each other at all. but he had a hunch that they were being prepared for a moment like this, and that the meeting point was Crisol, at that moment a nurse approached and took him out of his thoughts..

–Sir, your friend is fine, we have removed the bullet and now he is asleep and we have taken him upstairs to room three hundred and eleven.

–Thank you very much, could you speak to the hospital management? I have to consult a medical record from sixty years ago...

–Now it is not possible, the secretary only opens in the mornings at eight and until fourteen.

–Very good, thanks for everything, I'll be back in the morning, goodbye.

Inspector Borrull at that moment felt a strange emotion, he had a hunch that his life was going to change that a new world was opening up before him, aromas and perfumes, loves, and eternity, and above all, as always, war and blood. Everything that I had dreamed of when I was a child.

chapter 2

Universal love

The next day the inspector went to his workplace, the police headquarters, he had to present his report on the events of the last few days and his line of investigation entered the chief commissioner's office.

– Commissioner, with your permission, I bring you the written report on the attacks on the city's perfume shops.

–Very well, let me see, Wow, Borrull smells different today.

–That's right, I changed my brand of cologne.

–Well, I approve of my agents being clean and taking care of their appearance, but if you want advice, it is advisable not to overuse floral aromas because people talk and reach conclusions that could lead to misunderstandings about virility. Do you understand me?

–Of course sir, I will change my habits. Now I will go to the hospital to visit Agent Cusido, and at noon I will take a plane to Ibiza, I have a runway that takes me there.

–Of course, tell Agent Cusido to rest for a few days and be careful and be armed at all times.

-Of course sir! Thank you

The inspector left the office breathing with relief. He was afraid of the questions about the case and the police report. It could be said that the crucible perfume had saved him. Half an hour later he entered through the hospital door and went up to the room where the agent was. Cusido.

–Hello boy, how are you?

–Well, Mr. Inspector, they take wonderful care of me here, I knew that they give me peaches and pineapple in syrup for dessert.

–I see, you will have to rest here for a few days.

In the room, in addition to the nurses, there was the director of the hospital.

–Mr. Inspector, I am the administrator of the Amadeo Guillen hospital. I have been informed that you need a
medical report on a patient. As you know, that information is confidential even if sixty years have passed.

–Yes, yes, I know, it has nothing to do with any police investigation, it is a family issue, the person in question is my grandfather, and he died a few years ago. I would like to know what day he was admitted and when he was discharged, nothing more than that. For the family album it is just that, my mother would be very grateful.

–Well, if it is a family issue and the person is no longer alive, I don't see any problem, but you will have to give me a medical report that old for a few days, we don't have it here, it is archived in the medical school as a study from the beginning of the century, I will ask you to send it to me, tell the secretary the name of the person in question and we will notify you.

-Thank you and sorry for the inconvenience.

The nurses left the room with the director, leaving the two police officers alone.

–Albert, I'm going to Ibiza, I have to follow a trail that takes me to the Balearic Islands.

–I'm going with you, I'll get dressed right away.

–No, you don't have to stay in the hospital until you are discharged. I will inform you when I return, okay, and now take care, goodbye.

–Be careful sir, those guys are dangerous.

The inspector nodded and said goodbye by raising his hand.

Agent Albert Cusidó was a good boy, fresh out of the police academy, he was smart, had an agile mind and was helpful, he was a good assistant but it was necessary to hide the true reasons for his visit to Ibiza, it was better that way, because that case was closely related to his family and their quirky Botanical witchcraft friends.

He went out to the street and called a taxi, he had to go to the airport and meet Sevange and half an hour

Later he was in terminal number two at the ticket window when a hand touched his shoulder.

–Hello inspector, I have your ticket, let's go to the boarding area, our flight door is number twelve.

–If we have to work together we should call each other by first name, don't you think?

-That seems fine to me.

When they arrived at the control area, Inspector Borrull showed his police badge to the security members of the civil guard and they immediately let them pass without going through the magnetic arch, thus avoiding having to take the metal flask out of his pocket. of liquor and his

weapon. Once inside the plane, settled in their seats, they heard the pilot's voice telling them to take off.

–I'm curious why Angélica and Felix, their grandparents, didn't continue together. Do you know something Simon?

–Well, I spent many afternoons with my grandfather Felix and he never spoke to me because they separated, but I sense why, he came from a family deeply rooted in the

social traditions under the protection of the Catholic religion, and surely he wanted a normal, conventional family with a housewife wife, and all that about angels, witches, murderers, perfumes of destiny, astral travel and mysteries, it was very difficult for him to assimilate. Although I know that he loved my grandmother, he always spoke of her with admiration, I think he had to make a decision and that day had to be very difficult for him.

–And what do you know about your family, Sevange?

Not too much, they told me that they lived well in Barcelona until one day Spain went crazy and the civil war came, they had to return to China and we lived there for a

few years until China also went crazy and went to war with itself, and we left. Back to Spain, specifically to Barcelona, shortly after, my father died when I was a child, my grandfather took charge of my training in martial arts and the perfumed society instructed me in our magical and perfumed tradition. My father always told me about his mother, the delicate witch Severina, although he said that I looked like the feisty and determined witch Angelica. Curious, right!

–Ha, ha, ha, My grandfather Felix told me that I looked like Severina, that I was creative and intuitive like her. Strange! Right?

–Yes, true, it is possible that our families exchanged us, I would believe anything about them, but I have the eyes of my grandfather Wei.

At that moment the flight attendant approached, offering some glasses of orange juice that she was carrying on a tray. The inspector declined the invitation and put his hand in his jacket pocket and drank from the flask of liquor, a detail that did not go unnoticed. unnoticed by Sevange while she accepted the glass of orangeade. Minutes later the plane was preparing to land at Ibiza airport.

Once they got off the plane at the foot of the runway.

-And good? Where do we go now Simon?

−We will take a taxi and go to the island's police unit, it is the best place to gather information about the hippie communes and their ways of functioning.

After half an hour of driving around the island, the driver of the vehicle left them at the door of the police headquarters.

−Hello, good afternoon, I am police inspector Simón Borrull from Barcelona. Could I speak to the commissioner in charge?

The agent on duty nodded his head and indicated that he should follow him. They entered a large office with a very high ceiling. Once the introductions had been made, the commissioner invited them to sit down.

−I am Commissioner Rodrigo Garcia. Well, what do you say?

−Thank you, Commissioner, we come from Barcelona because we are looking for a girl named Estela Portabella and we know that she is staying in a hippie commune here on the island and I was wondering if you know what characteristics of some of them, for example, what economic means they have to survive.

−These people do not arouse our interest, they rent a large country house and they all live together, they eat from a

garden and sing songs in their trinket markets and little else, we only watch them when there is hashish and marijuana trading. We are much more concerned about the sects. nuns from abroad who want to capture our youth and destroy their souls, we monitor them very closely.

−I understand, Commissioner, you told me that they have a market, could you tell me which is the most important of these communes.

−The one from Punta Galera

−Thank you, Commissioner.

Inspector Simon and Sevange said goodbye to the Chief Constable and walked outside and Sevange headed to a car rental establishment.

−Do you want to rent a car? But we don't know where Punta Galera is.

–That's why Simon maps exist.

And immediately he took out a map of the island of Ibiza from his pocket, a fact that made Simon suspect that Sevange knew where to look even before taking the plane and meeting each other.

–Well, you drive and I will show you the way to follow, Simon.

After a short period of driving, they arrived at the Punta Galera cove, they stopped the car and saw through the window many people with little clothing and with smiling faces walking in different directions, they got out of the car and asked a girl with a ribbon in her hair, a flowered blouse and a happy face.

"Excuse me, miss, do you know a girl named Estela portabella?" Simon asked.

–All beings are like trails in the universe, we live in an ocean of love in freedom and...

–I understand, that's not it.

–Look, Simon, there on that road that leads to that castle there is a sign that says welcome to the "perfumed destiny." I think we have arrived.

–Perfect, let's get in the car.

Once underway it only took them five minutes of driving up a hill, the place was a large castle similar to an old military fortress, converted into a mansion with messages of love and peace on the walls along with a large expanse of land a Once they got out of the car, they were surprised that there was no door, instead there was a curtain of brightly colored beads, all very pop-hippie...

What happened to the gate? -Simon asked-Let's go in!

Once inside the lobby of the mansion they saw many mattresses scattered on the floor where a multitude of bodies of young people were sleeping.

between colored fabrics that hung from the ceiling and descended over the bodies like sheets.

–What are all these naked people doing sleeping at this hour? "And stacked on top of each other they look like cattle," Sevange asked in amazement.
–I guess they call this free love! Here I have a photograph of Estela, look at it Sevange

–I think it's that one, I recognize that perfume

–How can you know! here is a mix of patchouli and peppermint incense scents
–And hashish –completed Sevange
The girl called Estela was half covered with a thin ocher-colored sheet, lovingly hugging a boy and a girl,
each on one side of her naked body. She had light brown hair and skin golden from the Mediterranean sun. She slept with sunglasses. Sun with yellow crystals was the same age as them, about twenty-something years old. Even
while asleep, she had that something that defined her as an anarchic, idealistic and bossy person.

Suddenly a deafening noise similar to helicopter blades filled the room, causing most people to wake up. Sevange approached a window and watched as a group of men with military training descended some knotted ropes, landing on the roof of the building. castle.
–Some mercenaries are attacking us, wake up Estela!
Inspector Simon approached the still sleeping girl's face and screamed.
–Estelaaa wake up we are in danger.
–What the hell, but who the hell are you, and that noise? uffff my head is spinning...
Suddenly a t-shirt and shorts fell in his face, which Sevange threw at him forcefully.
"We are botanical witches like you, and now get dressed and run if you don't want to die..." Sevange ordered.

–These clothes are not mine, damn it! Who is this aunt? -Estela shouted-

For Estela, the words we are witches like you had a spring-like effect on her, she quickly placed her shirt over her shoulders while she looked at the two strangers who were urging her to follow them, without a doubt something serious was happening, while around her all the sleepy guests of Estela was getting up and running over each other, creating more confusion. They believed that the police were coming to arrest them. Sevange and Simon took Estela by the hand and ran up the stairs looking for a place to escape, at the same moment that the intruders entered, armed and uniformed and well trained accompanied by two men in suits with photographs in their hands, looking at the faces of the women who were there, it was clear that they were looking for someone and that someone was the botanical witch Estela.

–Come down this hallway we will reach my botanical study –Estela hastened to say.

Once inside, Estela grabbed a type of glass container with a dark greenish liquid. In turn, Inspector Simón took out his gun and Sevange tied his hair up with a ribbon ready to fight.

–Well, who are you? You know my name. And who are those guys?

–The explanations at the end, your grandmother Crisol sent us, my name is Simón and I am a police officer

–My name is Sevange, now we have to fight if we want to get out of here alive.

At that moment, knocks were heard on the door and later shots were heard. The studio had an exit to the outside where they were able to escape over the roofs while a group of armed men followed. Sevange lagged behind to

fight hidden behind a smoke vent from a chimney, which gave him an advantage, Simon stopped, he also hid,

pointing his gun to cover Sevange. In a few moments, the fight between both sides began, a shower of shots and blows caused many of the assailants to fall from the roof to the floor of the building. castle, meanwhile Estela, hidden, observed the scene for which she was not prepared nor for the feeling of admiration and annoyance because two strangers had saved her and she had not contributed anything to defend herself or help them, until now because she had the container of the green-mandrake perfume that would make anyone who inhaled it faint, recipe from his grandmother Crisol.

-Simon, Sevange, cover your face with your hands quickly -Estela shouted-

When he poured it into the air, the fluid spread in all directions but the result was not what was expected, no one fainted, but it did cause severe eye irritation and a persistent cough to everyone who was there, causing them to bend their knees and collapse. They will cover their faces with their hands, a moment that the three friends took advantage of to escape by jumping from the lowest part of the roof to the ground.

–Quickly run to the car, I'll go to the helicopter

–Nooo, come with us, forget about them.

But Inspector Simón did not want to flee without knowing who those guys were, he approached one of them dressed in a suit who was on the ground holding his leg with his hands, it was clear that he had broken it in the fall, He pointed his gun at his chest.

–Talk about who you are and what you want from us.

The man on the ground looked at him with disdain and did not seem to have any intention of speaking.

–Very well, how about I step on your leg...

The stranger let out a scream of pain.

Okay fuck it, we're an organization called Golden Skulls.

Give us the "Crimson Angel" and nothing will happen to you otherwise you will die.

At that moment the mercenaries stationed on the roof were recovering and were beginning to leave the castle.

–Simon gets into the car at once.

Sevange shouted, once the inspector got into the car, she started the car in a hurry, while the mercenaries entered the helicopter to chase them, and thus a chase along the road began, the attackers shot from above, Simon took out the flask from his jacket and took a long drink while loading his pistol with spare bullets.

"Shoot Simon at the fuel tank quickly," Sevange suggested imperatively. He didn't know where the hell that device had the fuel, so he fired shots at various parts of the engine, until suddenly a column of smoke made the

helicopter to move away from them and make an emergency landing hundreds of meters from where they were driving.

"Fucking bastards, does anyone want a drink?" Simon asked.

–I do need it, now you guys will tell me who you are and why those criminals were looking for me –Estela argued-what is this herbal potion, puafff?

While driving, Sevange looked at Simon and doubted that this crazy adventure would turn out well, in a few moments he stopped the car behind some bushes as a camouflage.

–Well, let's start, a few days ago some well-trained evildoers have been attacking us Botanical Witches. Simon and I are descendants of Angelica and Severina, you know who I'm talking about since you are Crisol's granddaughter. It was she who told us to go find you.

–In addition to being a police inspector, I am also a botanical perfumer, and I would appreciate it if you would use the masculine gender when you name me.

–In our tradition there are no witches, but we will get used to it, right Sevange?

–We'll see! Have you gotten information from the injured guy on the ground?

–Yes, they are from an organization called Golden Skulls, and they want us to give them the "Crimson Angel". Do you know anything about it? Because yesterday they tried to kill me, so no witch secrets.

There was an exchange of glances between them, distrust and fear floated inside the car, and the most worried was Sevange.

–I swear I don't know anything about it, I just want a lifc of peace and love on the island of Ibiza and now I'm leaving.

Estela opened the car door to get out, when Sevange stopped her by grabbing her arm.

–Stay here crazy, we are all in danger, those guys are looking for the three of us, they think we have the "crimson angel" but that is impossible.

–In masculine please, because you say it is impossible. What is the Crimesi Angel?

–Legend says that it is a very powerful ancient perfume, no one knows how to make it, only master botanical alchemists, the only person interested in these fragrances

was the dangerous Black Lady, she had an intimate relationship with some of them, such as the Count of Saint Germain, my ancestor. The perfume in question is not within the reach of mediocre people like you, you drink perfumes because they are not even useful for the nose of a cow and Estela almost blinded us a while ago with that fluid that... Wait, are you trying to imitate the famous Black Lady!? You wanted to knock those guys unconscious!

–Yes, yes, I'm a disaster as a witch, but you little girl, you're not much, the perfume you're wearing looks like cheap cologne, which means you only know how to hit people and...

–Fuck girls! That's it, you've forgotten that the three of us are in danger! We have to find out why that organization believes that we have that mysterious perfume, the next step would be to search for information and ask the scent archive of the Perfumed Society.

–Okay, but at this time of the afternoon there are no flights to Barcelona and the boat leaves early tomorrow, I propose we hide at the house of a friend of mine who

He is a medium, and well he could do a session in the world of the dead and invoke the Black Lady.

–Only a botanical witch from the forest can come up with such an idea. I remind you that the Black Lady is a murderous witch. Do you think she was going to help us because you are a fan of hers?

–I am not a fan of that woman, I make perfumes for peace and love between people and to advance in a better world.

–Ha, ha, ha, your grandmother was right, you are a naive person who plays at being a good person, ask Simón, who is a police officer, what world we live in.

–Please stop fighting, if our families saw us they would fight us out of fear. I remind you that we belong to a glorious, very ancient secret tradition and as such we have to honor it and help each other.

The two women looked at each other and nodded. It was not a time for discussions but for action and collaboration.

–Well, okay, let's go see Estela's friend.

Estela got out of the car and changed her position to the driver's seat and Sevange sat in the back seats of the vehicle. In a few seconds they started off.

–How is my grandmother Crisol, is she okay?

–Yes, I recently went to visit her at the nursing home and had a very interesting talk with her.

–Is my grandmother in a nursing home? Botanical witches do not enter those places, they take care of each other, this is very rare.

Simón and Sevange looked at each other, Estela was right, the Perfumed Society takes care of its members when they are older, there was something here that didn't fit.

–I think Sevange also spoke with her at the asylum, right?

–No Simon, I talked to Crisol at the perfume museum, that's where the Witches meet behind closed doors, he told me to protect you just a few days ago.

–Well, we will talk about that later now. We will go to the town of Sant Llorenc, where my friend Madame de

Malhues lives. She is a Chilean lysergic medium who will help us invoke the late Black Lady. It is possible that we will get information about magical perfumes, and perhaps pass the night at home.

The rest of the journey was in silence, each of them was immersed in their thoughts, they had to reorder the last events they had experienced. After traveling several kilometers they arrived at a house that had a facade painted in bright and cheerful colors. Estela stopped the car and parked it semi-hidden behind a gardener's shed near an orchard.

–Well, we have arrived, above all it is essential to humor my friend and don't anger her. She has a very peculiar character.-Estela stated.

They got out of the car and a few steps later they reached the door frame. After an endless minute, they rang the bell. The door was opened by a woman older than them, about forty years old. She was tall, dark-haired, with tangled and disheveled hair, and bright eyes. He was wearing an orange tunic with drawings of blue stars and excessively perfumed, he looked like a cartoon.

–What a surprise, Estela, I haven't heard from you in more than a year! Come in, come in. Are they your friends?

–Yes, they are Sevange and Simón and she is Madame Malhues

The hostess made an exaggerated bow, while the others only bowed their heads in respect, Simon looked around the walls of the house that were wildly painted in colors that seemed like a scream to the eyes while a song from a record played. group Four tops (Reach out for me) and to complete the props there was a mixture of smells of patchouli, orange incense and marijuana.

–Do you want something to drink or smoke? Angela's friends.

–Yes, thank you, I could use a brandy or cognac.

–And you dears?

–Anything will be fine, thank you. The reason for the visit is because we need your help and remember that my name is Estela and not Angela

–Of course, of course, but first sit down, I'll get the drinks and then we'll talk.

–Wow, he said "Angela's friends" he doesn't even remember our names and just a minute ago

that we have introduced ourselves. This is like a joke –Sevange commented distrustfully-

–Don't worry, Sevange, we need to spend the night here.

–Sure, Simon, okay.

After a few minutes, Estela and the hostess returned from the kitchen with a tray of drinks.

–So, you want to do a spiritualism session and communicate with a friend of yours who died years ago...

-Well. as much as a friend....

Estela winked with her eyes at Simon, so that he would not continue down that path. After a while of animated conversation, they entered a small room where there was a table in the center, with several glasses with candles inside. Once everyone was seated around them, they formed a circle and holding hands, the madame began to articulate words in a tone. in a trance while moving his head from one side of the table to the other.

–Quick, what was your friend's name?

–She was known as the Black Lady, a botanical teacher.

How was she known, don't you know her name and what she looked like? How do you want me to contact her, I'm not a fortune teller, I'm a medium! Do you have a photo of that woman?

–I'm afraid not, she was an ancestor of mine, we wanted to invoke her because we need information on an issue. I think it was a bad idea to come here, I apologize.

–Well, well if you are a relative of that woman at least we have something.

Madame Mulhaes tried again, repeating the same invocation but this time highlighting that there was a

relative of the late Black Lady. In a few seconds the madame's neck became rigid, her voice changed, her grave and rough tone became sweet and pleasant, with a calm rhythm like the voice of the Black Lady when she was alive, with an indefinite accent.

–Bonjour dears! Do you want to see me again?

"Ask quickly, I won't be able to last long, ufff," said the medium lady.

–My name is Simon, I am the grandson of the witch Angelica, we have called on you to help us, we need you to tell us about the Crimson angel and the Golden skulls organization.

The madame was sweating profusely, it seemed like she was trying to free herself from someone who was holding her prisoner. She tried to move her neck but an intense stiffness prevented her. The candles placed in the center of the table began to rotate at high speed, the large lamp that hung from the The ceiling swung like a frantic pendulum, the paintings broke in half, the windows were violently opened by an unknown force from outside.

– My dear sisters , come look for me and we will talk – the Black Lady recited as if in a litany.

The poor woman collapsed on the table, the session was over Estela, Simon and Sevange looked at each other, they had heard about that mysterious woman and were certain that they had contacted her, the accent, the mixture of languages, the confidence in Madame Malhues herself suddenly sat up and began to scream furiously, she felt deceived.

–Get out of my house, everyone, that woman is very dangerous, she almost possesses me completely, she is a witch, everyone get out right now I will have to clean all the negative energy that has entered my house... everyone leave!

The three quickly got up and headed to the exit door, at the same time Estela apologized for what had happened, but the hostess was worried about burning incense and throwing salt on the floor, she didn't even listen to the apologies, once outside the room. home and got into the car, Estela put the key in the ignition and started the car.

–Estela, are you angry?

–with myself, Simon! What a stupid idea I've had, today I lost a friend. Now I will leave you at the port, there you will find accommodation to spend the night and tomorrow you can take a boat and return to Barcelona.

–You're not coming with us?

–No Sevange, my path is not yours, nice to meet you and...

–I am very sorry for what happened in that house, but the point is that there is a group of murderers who are looking for us because they think that we have a magical perfume and only if we remain united will we be stronger and have a chance to survive.

–I don't see it that way Sevange, I know how to take care of myself. Well we have arrived.

Once the car stopped, the three of them got out of the car.

–I'm going to the maritime office to buy the tickets.

–Very well Sevange, tell me something Estela. Do you really think that a group of girls and boys singing songs of peace and love is more important than your botanical witch tradition.

–Simon, you are a police officer, you know very well that society is unfair to people and if someone has knowledge like ours, we must try to teach others to live in harmony with everything that surrounds us.

"Then we only have to return to Barcelona and tell your grandmother Crisol that we have failed to convince you to join us," Simón responded. At that moment Sevange joined the conversation.

–Very well, go with that group of friends and wallow in free love and the boredom of flowery shirts, but if one day you remember who you are we will be waiting for you, if you are still alive.

After those words Sevange turned around and went to the ship. Simon says goodbye to Estela with a kiss on the cheek and they wished each other luck, and while Estela walked away Simon climbed onto the ship

following in Sevange's footsteps, once on the deck of the ship he joined
her.

–We have to find accommodation to spend the night.

–I have bought cabin tickets, we will be safer there.

"It's a shame Estela didn't join us," said Simon.

–It is better to leave her alone to reflect on her priorities, the truth is
that we need her, she is a forest witch.

–Tell me Sevange, what is the difference between a city witch and one
from the forest.

–They taught me that city witches are refined, balanced and depending
on their ambition they can be brilliant or very dangerous women, and
forest witches are

unpredictable, fanciful and very imaginative but they have no
moderation or

stability that's why they called them "the crazy ones of the house"
no one dares to take a "flight" with them. Severina and Angelica our
grandmothers were city botanical witches.

"You mean we need imagination and passion," Simon concluded, and
Sevange confirmed with a nod of his head.

While Estela walked through the city towards her house, lost in her
thoughts, a doubt gnawed at her and if Sevange was right and it was
time to change her way of life, her friends in the hippie commune were
good people or maybe not, they were simply pacifists who did not want
to live like their parents, much less work themselves to death like them,
but they also did not have a clear idea of what they want to be and
much less a path to follow. And if my perfumes were not energetic at
all and did not bring progress to the hippie movement, I was in a sea of
doubts, it was time to take out the Tarot card that she always kept in
her cashmere bag, the Arcanum that belonged to her by date of birth
along with with its perfume "the Hanged Man" whose image is a man
hanging with a rope by his

feet, the meaning being the moment of a person when he changes his vision of everything that surrounds him and

the way of seeing life, the time has come to meditate on the past days of having another perspective, the false hopes, the broken illusions do not give any more, now it is time to humility and recognize that I was wrong. He took the perfume of his life and poured a few drops over his body.

Now it was starting to get dark and he had a decision to make, return to the commune with the others or fight against the Golden Skulls mercenaries with Simón and Sevange, at that moment a siren noise from police and fire cars forced him to turn his head. He looked back and looked at the top of the mountain where his family's castle-house was and saw that it was consumed by flames. The fire reached the turrets. In a few minutes, there would be nothing left of his house. At that moment he thought that this simplified the decision, in the end destiny rules.

While Sevange and Simón leaned on the railing on the side of the ship near the boarding ladder, they talked about the next steps to follow.

–I think that once in Barcelona we would have to go where the Perfumed Society meets and look for information. Do you think Simón?

–Okay, who is the teacher of the Society?

–Her name is Nuria Gaudí, she was a close friend of your grandmother Angelica. Wow, what a surprise, here comes Estela!

–Hello girls! Do you have a cabin for me? The fresh sea air will be good for me, it is very hot at home.

–Finally I will get used to being addressed in the feminine.

Estela and Sevange laughed at the same time that he took out a bill from his shirt pocket and showed her a show of hands. Estela made a gesture of approval and began to climb the boarding stairs.

"Let's go to dinner, I'm starving, you pay, I'm broke," Estela commented.

chapter 3

THE SECRET OF CRISOL

The boat trip lasted all night to travel the three hundred kilometers that separate Ibiza from Barcelona. In the cabin, Simon looked at the two girls who were sleeping like they were blessed, but he had trouble falling asleep, so he went to the bar to have a drink. a glass and fill his flask with liquor or better yet brandy once at the counter he spoke to the bartender.

–Hello, please give me a brandy, tell me the cabins with how many seats they have.

–Well, there are two and four-seater ones.

-Thank you!

Inspector Simon finished his glass while remembering his grandfather's words about botanical witches, "These women are special," and he always harbored the secrethope of meeting them. It was not surprising that Sevange knew that Estela would change her mind, which is why she

bought tickets. in a four-seater cabin, the possibility of meeting the The mysterious Black Lady was too attractive for an emotional Witch like Estela. She left the glass on the counter and returned to where her new friends were resting, she undressed and got into bed and in a few minutes she fell asleep.

–Simon wakes up, we have arrived at port, Sevange is waiting for us on the deck, he is monitoring possible suspicious movements.

–Of course, I have to go to the central police station and then maybe we should go visit Crisol or the Perfumed Society, after lunch of course.

–Okay, let's go.

Simon finished dressing and with Estela they headed to meet Sevange, once they all got off the boat together and entered a cafeteria in the port, where they ordered coffee with milk and strawberry cake.
–Well, now what we do, I hope you have a plan –said Estela.

–We have thought about visiting the Botanical Society to ask for information, but first I have to go through the police headquarters.

–Wait, do you know where the botanical witches meet?

–Yes, I have attended their meetings as a guest because I am Severina's granddaughter.

And where do they meet?

"Witch's secret," Sevange told him, narrowing his slanted eyes.

Once they finished breakfast, they took a taxi and headed to the police station and once they arrived, they climbed the stairs that lead to the offices. At that moment, agent Albert Cusidó appeared with his arm bandaged.

–Hello inspector, I have heard that there has been quite a commotion in Ibiza, do you have something to do with it?

–More or less. How is your shoulder, Albert?

–Well, the wound is healing, I will still be on medical leave for a few weeks, oh I wanted to tell you that I have the report of when your grandfather was admitted injured!I

knew that he had three bullet wounds in his body, he fell from twenty meters high and three days later he came out

of the hospital. hospital on his own! Was your grandfather made of iron?

Sevange and Estela looked at each other, they knew the story and it was not wise to stir that up.

–Oh no, Albert, there is an explanation. Look, when they made the report, they wrote the wrong month in June when in reality it was a whole month, they should have written July.

–Of course, of course that should be, and these ladies? You are the fighter!

–Yes, they are Estela and Sevange, they are childhood friends and related to my family.

Oh, I also wanted to tell you that the lady we went to visit at the nursing home, Crisol I think was her name, has died, the funeral is at noon today, in the Este cemetery in the Pueblo Nuevo neighborhood.

Estela put her hands to her face, sobbing, in an instant her memories as a child came to mind, of the years spent with her grandmother, the walks, the snacks in the Ciutat Vella park (old city), the magical stories about the witch she was

telling him, Simon put his arm around her shoulder as a way of comforting

–It was his grandmother, Albert, tomorrow I will pass the report to the chief director, now we are leaving.

–Don't worry, Mr. Inspector, I'll talk to the commissioner, and I'm sorry for being the bearer of such bad news.

They said goodbye to agent Cusidó and went down the stairs towards the exit door, and once on the street.

–It's strange how many times I spoke with Crisol it seemed to me that he was in good physical condition despite his age, the last thing he told me was Sevange protect my granddaughter and Inspector Simón. The three of you stay together if you want to survive, the magic phrase will come to you when you need it.

–You mean, my grandmother knew that a criminal organization is after us. How is that possible? What do they want from us? The magic phrase is only for a witch triangle! –said Estela surprised.

–The wounded mercenary I interrogated told me to give him the "Crimson Angel."

–You have a perfume store and you are in contact with the Perfumed Society, isn't that right Sevange?

–Yes, I have a perfume establishment called "Perfuman" I make tarot, yoga meditation and chakra opening fragrances. Here we are talking about a magical perfume, very old and it is not in our hands to make it, I don't know why they think we have it, and until a few days ago we didn't know each other.

–Good girls, now it would be better to go to Mrs. Crisol's funeral. We will buy some flowers on the way to the cemetery.

–Yes, thank you Simón.

Sevange made a sign with his arm and stopped a taxi after half an hour of travel with a stop at a flower shop included, they arrived at the eastern cemetery, one of the oldest in the city of Barcelona in the area of the Pueblo Nuevo neighborhood very close by. from sea. When they got out of the car, Inspector Simón saw that the place was heavily guarded by private detectives guarding the access doors to the holy field, all of them with weapons permits, some of whom he knew because they had previously been police officers. They approached the main entrance and one of the guards greet you. and shook hands.

–Hello Inspector Simon, how long, three, four years?

–Hello Andres, more or less, what is this function due to? -He said pointing with his arm.

–An association of ladies perfumers or something like that has hired us, which is why there have been serious mishaps with a gang of international criminals.

Sevange and Estela looked at each other, they assumed that something else had happened.

–I hope you didn't come for a familiar inspector.

–No, I'm not coming because of a friend who has died. Well, I'm glad to see you, Andres.

–Sometimes we meet to have a few beers with the guys from the class of sixties, if you want to sign up we will let you know.

–Of course, see you soon friend.

Once inside they walked through the central area, until they reached an alley with both walls full of tombstones, suddenly Simon stopped, he saw a newly married couple, he in a navy blue suit, she in a white wedding dress, the girl was talking to her dead mother on her wedding day, the emotion she felt, how happy she was, times that will be memories in a paper photo. He took out the flask from his pocket for the moments that required a good drink; that scene reminded him nostalgically of his grandfather's words.

"When there is hope everything begins again Simon"

Sevange and Estela, who were walking a few meters ahead, did not understand why Simon had been delayed when they retraced their steps and also saw the scene.

–Simon! Why do you stop?

–Because Sevange is a romantic

–Okay, come on girls.

Immediately they resumed their march, and a short distance away they saw a large number of women elegantly dressed in dark clothes. There was a priest reciting a prayer. Estela approached and placed a bouquet of flowers of various species in the coffin. She looked around and saw no one. of his family, a detail that seemed most strange to him. Sevange approached a lady who was in the center of the procession.

–Hello Nuria, is everything okay?

–Well, I could tell you that we have lived in better times, but that wouldn't be true, for one reason or another we have been burned, hanged, poisoned, kidnapped, murdered,

why continue, life doesn't smile on you either. Am I wrong, Sevange? ?

–We wanted to talk to you about this, what do you know about the Crimson Angel and the golden skulls.

–I'm afraid not much! Hello Simon and Estela, how you have grown up, I remember you from when you were children.

Regarding your question, the crimson angel is a powerful magical perfume from the alchemists of antiquity that we never wanted to know anything about, those fragrances only bring death and destruction, as for that criminal organization, the Golden Skulls, it comes from the ancient inquisitors and Witch hunters, eager to obtain all kinds of objects with magical powers.

–I think we should talk to the teacher of the scent archive to find out who made the perfume. Is she here?

–Yes, of course Simon, that's why we are here.

-And where is?

–The botanical teacher looked down at the coffin.

–My grandmother Crisol was the archive of aromas!

You already know Estela: Witch secrets! and now we're leaving we have to find a hole to hide, those guys have kidnapped three of our sisters, we have to come up with a plan of attack. Simon, if you know anything about your grandmother Angelica, remind her that it would be a great help at this time. She and I shared aromas and fragrances

in the past, but Angelica liked the company of Severina and Commissioner Felix more.

The workers finished placing the tombstone that covered the crypt while the numerous perfumed procession moved away.

–I propose to go to my house, I am a police officer, therefore my address does not appear in any record or file, by the way the botanical teacher Nuria Gaudí and my grandmother never worked together, I think she has lied to us.

–No, Simon, he wasn't referring to work, he meant that they were lovers –Estela commented.

-As?? You mean they...

-Men! –Sevange reproached.

The three returned to take a taxi that took them to Inspector Simon's house. When they entered the house, they saw that furniture and belongings were all scattered on the floors. The

house had been robbed, there was no furniture left standing, clothes were piled up on the floor. The floor, a leather sofa, was cracked in the center.

–So we will be safe here, right?

–Look at it this way, Sevange, since they have already been here they probably won't come back, right Simon?

–My greenhouse!

The inspector ran up the stairs to reach the attic where he had his collection of perfumes and bottles of essential oils, along with his exotic flora, everything was destroyed, scattered on the floors, the bottles of perfumes and essential oils broken.

–Don't worry, Simon, we will help you replace all of this, right Sevange?

–Of course, now we are a team!

–Thank you girls, at least the fridge is intact, I'll make something to eat. In half an hour they prepared a salad, and some chicken sandwiches with fried green peppers and tomato with fried onion rings (the so-called pepito) and a bottle of white wine. During the meal they spoke little, they were tired of the latest events, the afternoon was getting dark.

–I'm going to take a shower, I propose that we spend the night here and tomorrow we decide what to do, okay?

–Very well Estela, then I'll use the shower. What are you thinking Simon? You've been quiet for a while.

–There is something that doesn't add up to me, today in the cemetery the members of the Perfumed Society had to pour drops of perfume into the coffin as tradition dictates and yet they haven't done it.

–Well, it is possible that they have forgotten – Estela mentioned.

Sevange was paralyzed, she knew that something like that was not possible, she stared at Simón.

Is there anything else that seems strange to you, Simon? –asked Sevange.

–Yes, when I went to visit Crisol in the residence, I could swear that the nun who opened the door to me smelled of perfume and the director was also scented with aromas that are recognizable to me, and in the conversation with

Crisol, she told me that witches botanists take care of each other. So what was she doing in a nursing home alone?

–I already told you that, in Ibiza, remember? -Estela confirmed.

–Come on girls, I have the car on the sidewalk in front.

–Eh, eeeh, wait to go where, right now I was going to take a shower – Estela commented –

–In the cemetery we have to open Crisol's tomb.

–Wow, you've gone crazy! It's my grandmother! I am not going to desecrate his grave and neither are you, I forbid it! -said Estela energetically.

–Tell me something Estela. Because there was no one from your family in the cemetery, doesn't it seem strange to you? –Sevange asked.

He had to admit that it was true, although his grandmother was mysterious and extravagant and lived life by her own rules, in these cases family always appears. And there was no one at the funeral.

–Well, okay, let's go to the cemetery. To hell with the shower!

"We're going to smell worse than the dead," Estela said energetically.

They went out to the street towards the car. When they arrived, Simon opened the doors of the vehicle for them to get in and once inside, in a small drawer on the car's dashboard, he took out the firearms that he kept there.

–Do you know how to use them?

–Yes, my father was the secretary of a sports shooting range –Sevange stated.

–Great, two days ago I was singing songs of peace and love and now I'm going armed to attack a cemetery.

Sevange and Simon looked at each other and smiled, they knew from the stories they had told them that the witches of the forest have an unpredictable destiny.

The journey took them thirty or forty minutes. Darkness had taken over the city and it was nine at night.

–We have arrived and the door is closed, well let's go! "No?" asked Estela.

Simón and Sevange surrounded the wall of the cemetery, the part that faced the sea, that way they would not be seen. Estela followed him a few meters further back,

shaking her head in disapproval, because she was afraid of what she was thinking. Her grandmother Crisol explained to her years ago. that they had to steal a corpse in the company of Severina and Angelica and the grandchildren were going to do something similar now. Arriving at a halfway point on the wall, the two girls joined their hands as an easel so that Simon could rest his foot and reach the part high of the wall, once sitting on top he extended his arm and pushed Estela up and between the two of them

they helped Sevange to climb, once the three of them were at the top of the wall they jumped inside.

–Well, we're inside, now if I'm not mistaken we have to go in that direction and look for my family's mausoleum – Estela stated.

At night the cemetery was even more Gothic if possible, the statues of angels and deceased people mixed with the dim light of the streetlamps seemed like a dance of trembling shadows. After a few minutes walking they arrived at the indicated place.

–Well, we have arrived at the pantheon, luckily the tombstone is newly fitted, it won't be very difficult to open it, let's all push from one end –Simon proposed.

–Wow Simon, it seems like you do this every day. What enthusiasm! -Sevange commented-

After pushing the tombstone that sealed the tomb, they placed it on the ground....

–Damn, how heavy this stone is! If you're wrong, Simon, we'll settle the score, ufff! - Estela commented annoyed.

–Stop complaining, and shut your fucking mouth – Sevange harassed angrily.

-This is too much! "I can't stand it when a Chinese woman shouts in my face, I'm leaving," Estela shouted angrily.

–Wait, calm down both of you, we are in the final part, we just have to check that Crucible is inside this coffin, and please don't scream.

After a few seconds of silence they lifted the closure of the coffin and.....

-But how! My grandmother Crisol's body is not there, you were right, Simon.

–The whole funeral was a farce! -Simon murmured.

–However, inside there is a rose and a written note, which says "In the winged square, the crossed witch, on the silver road" I think this message is for us.

"Now we better leave, we have to reflect on this," Sevange proposed.

They replaced the closure of the coffin and the slab on top and in silence they left the crypt and when they went to the

outer wall they heard voices in English of men approaching in the direction where a few minutes before they had been, they quickly hid behind some graves, those men, some dressed in elegant suits and others in military field uniforms, visit the family pantheon of Crisol. From a safe distance the three observe the scene

–Do you have any idea who these guys are, Simon?

–They are accompanied by the cemetery employee which means that they are accredited for anything, I think they are foreign secret services, they speak English with an American accent, this matter is becoming more and more complicated – Simon stated.

–It seems that they are leaving, it was just a check, I think they knew that my grandmother was the archive of aromas, they have not opened the tomb, it would be better that way –said Estela, relieved.

Minutes later they found a ladder that was used to clean the niches built into the cemetery wall, which they used to

go outside and once outside the cemetery they got into the car and drove to Inspector Simon's house.

–We will go to my house, since it has already been attacked we will be safe there.

–Imagine how what you said calms me down! –Estela expressed.

–No, Simon, those guys from the cemetery have followed us, I'm sure they're watching your house as much as mine. I propose that we get on a night tram and spend the night there.

–How? We have to sleep on a tram! –Estela asked in amazement.

-Yeah! walking around the city all night, that's what I did when my perfume store was robbed," Sevange said.

–I think it helps us that foreign secret services are watching us, and I am also sure that they were the ones who searched my house. They cut my sofa exactly in half on purpose to cover up what they were looking for. We will indirectly be protected by them from the Golden Skulls order.

"I support Simon's idea," Estela said relieved.

–We have to get used to moving on a tightrope. Tell me Sevange why do you think the Botanical Society has set up this farce, you have had dealings with them –said Simon while driving the car.

–As you know, the Botanical Witches are being attacked, not just the three of us.

"You mean you two and me," said Inspector Simon, raising his eyes to the roof of the car.

–Yes, well, I mean that they are protecting the Aroma Archive, which is Estela's grandmother, by making it look like she has died. The nursing home, the funeral, the

written note, all of this is a protection maneuver, I think that from now on we are alone against everyone-said Sevange.

-Brilliant! It was meeting you and my entire philosophy of life went to hell in two days!

"Our ancestors had it much worse, so don't complain," Sevange shouted furiously.

–I have assumed it and don't make me angry, little girl –Estela shouted.

–Come on, let's not lose our nerves, once we get home we will drink a bottle of wine and talk calmly about that message inside the coffin, I think it is the next step to follow.

"Okay, peace on my part," Estela proposed.

–For my part too – Sevange agreed.

Once the car was parked, they went up to Inspector Simón Borrull's attic apartment. He opened the door, gun in hand, to make sure that no one was inside, the house was still the same, everything on the floors, clothes, furniture, nothing had changed, although it seemed strange, it was reassuring. Simon prepared some sandwiches with priorat wine. "Very good, Simon, thank you for dinner and now I'm going to shower and go to sleep, tomorrow we'll talk good night," Estela said goodbye.

chapter 4

Crazy people and vampires

The next morning they gathered in the living room around a table with cups of coffee and muffins.

Let's look at the note we found yesterday in the cemetery, it says "The Witch's Cross, In the Winged Square" – I don't know what it means, Simon commented.

–Crisol was annoyed by witches' little secrets and in the end he fell into the same habit, but I think it is a message for us – said Sevange.

–I believe that the word "winged" refers to an angel, which would be the name of this square –said Estela, pointing with her finger at a map of the streets of Barcelona.

Simón and Sevange looked at each other strangely at the change in attitude.

They went out onto the street, got into the car and in a few minutes they arrived at the indicated place.

–Look, this is the Plaza del Ángel and on the façade of that building there is a statue of a woman, probably a botanical witch. She has a silver cross on her head, and as you know, silver is the metal of witches if we draw a straight line. From the cross, from here it takes us to that street called Silversmith's. Until here, everything fits together," Sevange expressed confidently.

They crossed the square and walked along the silver street that led down towards the port.

–And now we are supposed to go somewhere but where? The message ends here – commented Simon

–No Simon, the statue of the botanical witch had a cross in her hair.

-And?

–Well, it's a sign, and at the end of the street there is a church. Do you see the relationship? "We have to go in there," Sevange stated.

–Sevange is right, what better place for a witch to hide than a church, no one will look for her there – Estela assured.

"Wow, I have to admit that your resources are brilliant," Simon commented in amazement.

The church in question was the Basilica Santa Maria del Mar, built in the fourteenth century with the help of local fishermen who brought stone from a nearby quarry on Montjuich Mountain. (Jewish Mount) They entered through the temple gate, they walked along the side of the temple seeing the images of the saints and adjacent chapels. They were about to finish the tour until Estela saw in a hidden corner a small rusty iron door as old as herself. Church approached it and observed a drawing engraved on the top of a door.

–Wow, what we have here, look at this, the drawing on this door is a perfume bottle with a rose inside and the initials SP (Perfumed Society) – Estela commented.

Now they were clear that they were following a plan hatched by someone or something. They looked around them looking for the furtive glance of something or someone spying on them while they looked at the door without deciding to enter when behind them watching was the priest of the church.

"That door is waiting to be opened," said the priest.

Everyone turned their heads in amazement and stupor as if they were afraid of being discovered at the same time that Estela let out a small scream at the sudden comment.

–We're sorry Mr. Priest, I'm the police inspector, my name is Simón Borrull and well this door has caught our attention, but right now we're leaving, excuse me.

–If the path takes us to the threshold, what is the next step? "Misses Sevange and Estela," the priest commented in a low voice.

They looked at him in amazement, that man knew their names, without a doubt the priest came out to meet him and it was not by chance.

"Enter, of course," Estela responded.

–Well, here is the key, goodbye.

–Wait sir, what is your name, sir....

The mysterious character turned his head and smiled in a friendly manner as he walked away.

–Who is that man and since he knows our names – Estela pointed out – Sevange has not surprised you at all, right!

–Very easy, that priest was officiating at your grandmother Crisol's funeral, he is a member of the Perfumed Society,

some time ago male followers entered, times change, and now how about we enter.

They opened the door by turning the key as old as the rusty iron of the portal, a few centimeters away there was a staircase of stone steps in the shape of a spiral within a narrow corridor that rose upwards, they climbed numerous steps until they reached the end where another A door that was just as old and rusty as the previous one blocked their way, but this time it was not locked. They waited a few seconds with bated breath, looked at each other, pushed the door and entered a spacious and beautifully decorated room with shelves in The walls were full of bottles of essential oils and perfumed fragrances, flowers and plants preserved in a fluid that they could not identify, Asian lamps, large Turkish rugs, couches, paintings of angels and witches, and in one corner of the room there was a bed of the century XVIII. But there was something else that caught their attention.

–What a beautiful place, I think I would stay here – Estela commented in wonder.

–I highly doubt they would allow you to celebrate your crazy hippie parties here –Sevange stated.

The three approached a table that was in the center of the room and on it he had placed a baroque-style perfume bottle.

–Wow what we have here! A perfume. What do you think?

"I think they left it here on purpose for us to use," Sevange proposed.

–The person who left us the message now leaves us a perfume as a sign that will help us contact the Black Lady – Estela assured.

Sevange uncovered the closure of the bottle and each of them spread the perfume fluid throughout the body.

-It's strange, the aroma is familiar to me, it has something wild and ancient teucrium marum, mint, smilax aspera, and another ingredient that I can't quite identify and mugwort oil - Estela explained.

"I don't know what's wrong with me, I suddenly got hot and anxious," Simon said uneasily.

"And I'm very nervous, something's wrong with me," said Sevange, upset.

-My God! The ingredient is horse semen. It is a powerful aphrodisiac, the perfume is a filter of love, let's run, there's a quick shower there! —said Estela with labored breathing.
The three of them undressed in a hurry and got naked into the shower, which was a bad idea, the water does not

cancel out the effects but rather amplifies them and if they were also naked, it is easy to guess what came next, a waterfall of kisses. , caresses, hugs.

In a state of intoxication they heard a melodious voice

" LET MY PERFUME EXPLORE YOUR NAKED BODY, PENETRATE INTO THE SKIN, CARESS IT AS A STUNT LOVER WOULD DO, WITH THEIR EYES, THE FINGERS, THE LIPS. LET MY FRAGRANCE CORRECT YOUR SOUL "

They ran to the bed where they continued the erotic-sexual ecstasy for several hours until they fell asleep relaxed and satisfied... And satisfied. It had gotten dark when Simon's eyes began to open, he couldn't see clearly, but when he managed to focus his eyes he saw that he was naked, hugging Sevange, who in turn had his arm around Estela, and that they were still asleep. He tried to turn his head forward. and he saw the face of a woman appear, looking at him in surprise, it was Crisol. Simon waved the bodies of Sevange and Estela with his hand.

–Ehhh, what's happening, my God, we're naked. What happened? Melting pot! –Sevange commented surprised.

–Earth swallow me and I with this aunt. Oh my goodness, it was an accident. Grandma? Damn grandma, what story is this?

"Simon, Simon, I told you that the three of you had to form a magic triangle and not a love triangle," Crisol said with amusement.

–!Crisol! You are alive and much younger, how is it possible? –Simon was surprised.

–It's true, grandma, it seems like you're only fifty years old.

"Okay, okay, stop talking and please have someone hand me my clothes," Sevange said, uncomfortable with the situation.

–Okay girls, here you have your clothes, when you are visible we will talk about everything that happened, except for this of course. I'm going to make coffee, ahh here's the love filter that I forgot at the table yesterday, I had a date with a man and... well, I think I'm getting older and forgetting things.

The three looked at each other with a gesture of resignation.

–It is better not to talk about what happened, it was an accident and that's it –Estela agreed.

Sevange and Simón shook their heads in affirmation. Once they had dressed, they sat at the table and drank the coffee prepared by Crisol.

–I am satisfied that you will discover that the funeral was a farce, it was necessary to protect me as the Aromas archive that I am and since you have deciphered the message that I placed in the coffin, here I am to answer your questions.

I'll start well, Grandma! How is it possible that you are so young, you look the same as I remembered you years ago and you are over eighty.

–eighty-seven to be exact, as I explained to Simon a few days ago at the residence, the botanical witches Severina and Angelica took care of me when I was very sick, many years ago, they perfumed my body with the fragrance of the bottle where I had Having deposited the Emerald of the angel

Luzbel, the perfume acquires the power of the stone of youth, the same perfume that saved your grandfather's life, right Simon, now you understand why he did not have any scars on his body. Commissioner Felx Borrull was a warrior, a fighting man and he did not like the map of his wounds in combat disappearing from his skin, he did not

belong to our world and shortly after your mother was born. Angelica and Felix separated.

Who are the "Golden skulls" and what do they want from the three of us – Sevange asked.

–Well, that is more complicated, a few centuries ago some witch hunters and some inquisitors founded this order with the purpose of appropriating the relics of power, above all they want the knowledge of the manufacture of the perfumes bequeathed by the Angels to the witch. Bruxelle, for example "The Crimson Angel" we have been at war with them for hundreds of years, now they want to capture you three.

–And why us? –Simon asked.

–Because according to the ancient chronicle you have that perfume.

Sevange got up from the chair, nervously walking around the table while looking at Estela and Simon, who in turn looked at each other.

–Like we have it! Until today I had never heard of him, and until a few days ago I didn't know these two - said a surprised Simon.

–Grandma, explain that story to us, because I don't understand anything!

–I don't know much more because it hasn't happened yet, you and the black lady will fight against "the golden ones."

skulls" and you will get the famous perfume, that is why they are chasing you now.

–Wait, wait grandma! You say that the three of us and a dead witch will fight in the future with that gang of criminals and recover the "Crimson Angel" and you say that is something that has not happened yet. So, why are they chasing us now?

–Because that happened in the past, not in the future.

"They are chasing us through a past, in which we have not been, but what madness is this," Sevange shouted, very upset.

Crisol got up from the chair and approached Sevange who was trembling nervously.

–Sevange, Sevange calm down dear, remember that you are named after two formidable witches Severina and Angelica, you fear not being able to protect Estela and Simon and that scares you, but remember that you are the Force" on your date of birth in the Tarot Arcanum . You are disciplined, you have firmness of character and courage

in the fight, a winner in the physical and subtle world, with ethereal beauty and a flexible spirit, you must trust yourself more, dear, when you have doubts, remember your fragrance.

"Wait, wait, crucible! You just said that all of this happened in the past. What date are we talking about?" Simon asked.

–I think in 1780 or 1790, more or less.

Simon looked at both sides of the table, searching for his jacket pocket. That information deserved a good drink. Hours before that meeting he had thought about stopping drinking, but today was not the day.

–Humm, I see that you have changed the liquor for the brandy, pass me the flask,...Ahhh this is something else, I was sick of mass wine- Crisol exclaimed, relieved.

-Grandmother! And how are we supposed to go to the past with a time machine?

–I don't know, I hope you explain it to me when you come back, if I'm still alive.

–I don't know of any "flight" to the past with the physical body, only Severina and Angelica did it and in an astral way," Sevange assured.

–That's because "The Madwoman of the House" has never been attempted with a botanical witch from the forest – Crisol explained, looking at Estela.

–One more question Crisol: Did we return from that crazy mission? –Simon asked.

–Surely yes, there is a gang of criminals out there chasing you for something you still don't have. Oh yes! Don't bother looking for an explanation for this contradiction, theoretical

physicists call it the time paradox, botanical witches call it the mystery that is out there, it's that simple and normal.

And one more thing, my dears, when you find the Black Lady, do not forget that she is very dangerous, her great beauty, her suggestive and sweet voice, plus everything that woman has experienced, make her an irresistible and deadly woman.

–You mean that we have to go look for her in the kingdom of the dead but I don't see how we don't have a photo of her and we don't know what face she had-Sevange observed.

"Ehh, ehh, I'm not going to become a necrophile witch," Estela expressed, upset.

"It's called a Necromancer," Sevange stated.

–Well, in some way you have done it, it is part of our history as I have already explained.

–Remember that in Ibiza we contacted her through a medium –said Simon.

–There you have it, you have opened a road, and it is surely waiting for you to go.

–We need to know what perfume was the Black Lady's so she can take us to her–said Sevange.

-I know it.

Simon got up from the chair and went to the shelf where the tarot perfumes were and took out one of them, which he held up and showed the others which one it was. The fragrance of death.

Crisol nodded his head at Simon's choice.

–And now, dears and dear, I am leaving, be very careful and may good fortune be with you. And above all, behave

well in bed, remember that you are in a church – Crisol laughed loudly –

–When Crucible advanced towards the door and Sevange and Simon were talking to each other, Estela ran towards her.

–Wait grandma! I have to ask you something, the perfume that was on the table, the "love filter" was not accidental, it was deliberate, right?

–Well, you three don't know each other, and you can't face a dangerous mission under those conditions, so I thought that a few hours of passion unites more than anything, right?

–What a beast you are, grandmother!

–This is how we forest witches are, dear granddaughter. Take care!

Once Crucible had left, the three of them sat around the table looking at each other and at the perfume that was on top of the board in an atmosphere of uncomfortable silence. Sevange got up and went to a shelf where the cards of the major arcana of the tarot were and separated the death card and placed it next to the perfume that corresponded to a curse on the black lady.

–The time has come to "flight" into the unknown and search for the Black Lady in the kingdom of the dead – Sevange exclaimed vehemently.

–Okay, I'll start, I'll spread a few drops over my body, the lower abdomen is where we have our energy center, and now the next one, Estela commented.

–I will do the same as Estela but a little higher than the navel- Sevange followed.

"My strong point is intuition, so I'll put the fragrance on my chest near my heart," Simon continued.

–My mother! How mysterious this perfume is and at the same time attractive, I will concentrate on her voice. Now we hold hands, we close our eyes and remember that I direct the "flight." Don't let go of my hand. Do you have something to say? Okay, let's go then, I consider. Wake

After several minutes of silence and darkness, a fog seemed to take over the room, at the same time screams were heard in an indefinite distance, until the image where they were found became clearer, suddenly they saw themselves with the body rolling around on the floor. meters along the hard stone floor, when they opened their eyes they realized that they were no longer in the secret room of the church, they were in a very old vaulted

basement, on one of the side walls they saw a stone staircase.

"Damn, what a way to fly, my whole body is sore," said Sevange.

-Where we are? -Simon asked, touching an eyebrow that was bleeding.

"They look like the basements of a great castle, let's go up those stairs quickly," Sevange ordered.

–It's incredible, we did it! –said Estela amazed.

"The incredible thing is that we are alive with this entry we have made," Sevange responded, rubbing his purple knees.

– Don't be late Estela, we must stay together – Simon assured.

When they reached the end of the stairs and opened the door, they found themselves in a large, poorly lit room with exposed stone walls blackened by dirt, and in the middle of a Dantesque scene, men and women running screaming, they saw some burly men trying to restrain them with belts. Tied to some poor unfortunates who were screaming in pure panic, there were rooms with barred doors that looked like cells.

"What's going on here? What place is this?" Simon said.

"What a horrible place," commented Estela, disoriented.

A man with a wavy mustache and a white coat who looked like a doctor from the last century approached them.

-Who are you! What are you doing here?

–I am Inspector Simón Borrull, we come to look for a lady who calls herself...

–Get out of here! The inmates have become unhinged and some have escaped from their cells, here they are in danger and...

The doctor did not finish the sentence when his head exploded from a strong blow given to him by a man armed with an iron bar with a disfigured face and a look of pure madness, splashing blood on Estela's face.

"Let's get out of here, this place is a mental sanatorium," Sevange shouted.

The three friends ran up the stairs but a sick man with a torch in his hand blocked their path.

The man tried to hit Sevange with the firebrand, Sevange in a quick evasive maneuver tilted half of his body, and the man of his own momentum fell over the railing at the top of the stairs towards the ground. They were on a higher floor, they ran down a hallway that led to another large room, the whole place was a labyrinth of corridors, hallways and rooms, they didn't know where to go no matter where they looked, suddenly they saw a large group

of mentally ill people in In a state of madness, they savagely beat the guards and nurses.

–Where have you brought us Estela? –Simon shouted scared.

-Don't know.

"Now that doesn't matter, we have to get out of here, the rooftops are our only way out," said Sevange.

–Let's go up that staircase again to the top floor. I see a large window and there will be the door to the roofs of this place. "I'm very sorry for bringing you here," Estela announced worriedly.

When they reached the top floor, the scene was much worse. A large pack of wolves attacked the inmates of the sanatorium. The entire floor was a pool of blood, where a flock of bats flew around the room and drank the blood from the floor. Simon took out the gun. of his jacket, Sevange and Estela imitated him, with their backs pressed against the windows they tried to reach the door, Simon turned his head outside and saw something that scared him

even more, a man with a black cape was crawling up the exterior façade and red in the middle of a strong storm, of lightning and thunder accompanied by two women in gauzy white nightgowns and skin whiter than snow.

–Sevange, Estela, look down there, that's terrifying. Damn!

At that moment everything was perfectly clear to Estela, she now knew where they were, but the situation in which they found themselves had become more dangerous, the wolves and bats had realized their presence and were approaching them in a threatening manner, they were cornered.

–My God, now I know where we are and I'm really sorry for bringing you here, The Black Lady is not in this place.

And where are we! -Simon shouted as he pointed his gun at the wolves.

–In reality, this place does not exist, it is a creation of my imagination. I am a fan of vampire movies, and everything that is happening here is a scene from the movie Dracula – Estela commented worriedly.

-Oh! "Now I know who bit me on the neck the other afternoon at church," Sevange said with surprise.

"Let's run to the door while we shoot or we won't exist either," Simon shouted in fear.

The three opened fire at the same time they reached the entrance to a small room, where they locked themselves with a medieval lock, at which time the wolves fiercely hit the door with their heads, making the door creak and crack.

"We have to quickly bar the door with that closet," Simon exclaimed.

This room is not the exit to the roofs, it has no windows. We are screwed! –Sevange expressed with concern.

Estela searched in a pocket for the black lady's perfume, spreading the fragrance on Sevange and Simon and finally on herself.

– Now sit with me on the floor and give me your hands, I have to get you out of here.

"Very well Estela, I'll help you," said Sevange.

The three friends closed their eyes, Sevange put his mouth close to Estela's ear and whispered to her the magical phrase of the Botanical witch "Forget, dream, everything begins again" repeated several times, moments later the door broke into a thousand pieces as the man entered.

vampire and the wolves, but Estela Sevange and Simón were no longer there.

Chapter 5
The Home of the Black Lady

On this occasion the flight was not much better than the first time, they fell into a lake of warm, motionless water and covered in a thick mist that impedes visibility. When they managed to get their heads out of the water, they saw that none of the three could locate each other. , and shouting each other's names could be a dangerous option when you are in an unknown place until it occurred to Estela that if she thought about Simón and Sevange in emotional terms, the power of the love filter would attract them to her shortly after like this occurred. Although something strange happened to Sevange, the water reached his chin and there was an expression of immense sadness on his face, shortly after swimming and reaching her.

–Sevange! come give me your hand are you okay? What's the matter?
– I don't know, I have no strength or courage for anything, this place is very sad. I can barely see the fog, it's very thick, and Simon?
–Let's go look for him, don't let go of my hand.
In a few minutes they found Simón who was signaling to them with his hand. When they gathered they saw the shore that allowed them to get out of the water. Once stretched out on the ground...
–In the future, when we have time, we should perfect the landing technique for these "flights" – Simon said, laughing.
"I promise to do better in the future," Estela responded, laughing and raising her right hand.
–Thank you Estela for rescuing us from the water –Sevange thanked.
–You want to know how I did it! Estela was quick to say.
–Nooo! -Sevange shouted energetically.

"We have also noticed your desire and feeling for us," Simon said, smiling into Estela's ear.

–Well, well, I better keep quiet.

–Tell me Estela, how is it possible to take a "flight" to a place in your imagination like that asylum? "It's not supposed to exist," Simon asked as they lay on the floor.

–I have no idea, and I'm still scared because I didn't know I could do something like that.

–My grandmother, the witch Severina, explained to me in a dream that there is a very fine line between what is lived and what is dreamed and sometimes both worlds get confused,

which is why balance is important in the life of a witch –Sevange concluded the song.

–Does your grandmother Severina communicate with you in dreams? -Simon asked in amazement as he looked at Estela.

Sevenge did not answer, he just tilted his head to the side, pretending that he did not have an answer to that question, and after standing up and walking in the darkness.

-Where are we now? "We've been walking for a while and all we can see is a thick fog that moistens my face," Simon said, annoyed.

"I don't even see the ground I'm stepping on, I don't know if I'm going up or down, it looks like a limbo," Estela commented.

"We don't know, Simon, but I notice a dark presence that watches and stalks us," Sevange said fearfully.

"I've felt it too, but I didn't want to scare you," Simon commented worriedly.

At that moment they were advancing hand in hand and looking at all sides of the road, each suspicious noise and distant cry made them turn their heads in fear.

"I swear this time I concentrated on the voice and fragrance of the botanical witch we met at the seance," Estela protested.

Shortly after, they saw on the horizon the silhouette of a large baroque-style house with spiral turrets. On the threshold of the door the image of a woman was drawn, which became clearer as they approached, when they reached a few meters away. her.

–Welcome my dears! You have come to look for me, I am all yours.

-You are the?

Before Sevange finished the sentence, the woman bowed as was done during the Renaissance. She was the famous Black Lady that they had heard so much about since Estela and Sevange were children. They could barely breathe because of the emotions of fear and admiration that she aroused. the presence of that beautiful and mysterious woman.

"There is no doubt that it is her, I have never seen such a beautiful woman in my life," Simon said in amazement.

-A man! This is indeed a surprise, many things have changed since I was no longer alive, but please come to my humble abode.

–Simon, we are not so bad either. Man! -Estela commented annoyed, closing his mouth with her hand.

Once inside the three friends looked in all directions of that room, everything seemed so strange to them. The decoration of the walls was done with exquisite taste, the fireplace was lit, although

Outside the house it was neither cold nor hot, in the center of the room a sumptuous table full of food and drink, surrounded by luxurious couches.

–How about we make the introductions! I am the black Lady as you already know

–My name is Sevange, I am Severina's granddaughter, and this is Estela and Simon

–Simon, you look a lot like my descendant, the Botanical Witch Angelica, are you an alchemist or a witch? and this young woman here I imagine is the granddaughter of the woman who killed me.

"It was in self-defense, you wanted to stick a dagger into Severina's body," Estela said elegantly.

–It's true cheri! They were moments of madness and some disagreements over a stolen object, but hey, we are a family and these things happen," the black lady said conciliatoryly.

–We have come to look for you. But what place is this? Where are we? There is a dark and threatening presence out there.

–Believe me Simon when I tell you that I don't know, maybe an intermediate place between heaven and earth or

hell. The power of the emerald of the Angel of beautiful light (Luzbel) immersed in my perfume that I have carried for hundreds of years has created this place for me once I leave the world of the living. I believe that the presence that you have noticed outside this house is something sinister that wants to capture me and take me to I don't know what place, but for some unknown reason it cannot enter here. Alora if you want to eat and drink you are invited.

The three of them declined the offer, keeping Crisol's words of warning about the host's danger in mind, although for Simon the temptation of a good glass of brandy was very great, especially after what he had experienced in the mental sanatorium they left behind.

"The truth is that I need a good drink, you don't know how difficult it has been to get here," Simon stated.

The black lady served drinks for everyone, and was the first to drink, the others followed her, Sevange spoke up to explain why they had come to look for her.

–We have come because the members of the Perfumed Society and we are being attacked by an organization called "Golden Skulls." They believe that we have a perfume called "the Crimson Angel."

-I know it! Do you have it?

-Of course not! We hardly know anything about the power of that fragrance or what effects it produces, but they persecute us because according to the other botanical witches we have traveled to the past with you and we got hold of it. It's crazy, really! -Estela commented.

The Black Lady rose like a spring from the couch and stood up, raising her fists in euphoria and shouting.

–Mon dieu! I'll finally get out of here.

–So will you help us? -Simon asked.

–Of course, you are my family!

–Well, make yourself comfortable on the couch because the story is very long, by the way. Do women wear such short and wet dresses in your time?

–Yes, they are called Mini skirts and we are experiencing a cultural and sexual revolution –Estela boasted.

–Ahh, the revolutions, I remember Versailles... Anyway

The Black Lady remained silent with a lost look, it seemed that she remembered something beautiful and sad at the same time.

"You said you were going to tell us a story," Sevange continued.

-Yes of course! A long time ago, as a teacher of the Perfumed Society, I met a very special man called the Count of Saint Germain. He was a

magician, an alchemist, and a keen conversationalist. He had a sense of existence that was provocative at that time. He came from a very ancient family. Knowledge in alchemical botany was one of the most mysterious and attractive as everything he was. We were close friends, yes well also lovers, at that time the young magician alchemist Cagliostro had a disciple-assistant, a close charming man, different from his master and so identical to him! The dear truth is that this type of men are the only ones who they're worth it! Well, let's continue, the aforementioned Count Saint Germain had an ancient parchment, written in the language of angels, it was known as "The Lucis Spell" in which it explains how to make the famous Crimson Angel perfume.
–And what effects does that magical perfume have? –Simon asked.
–My dear Simon, you will see that for yourself, and what is more important, you should not look into the eyes of the person who is wearing that fragrance.
–What can happen to us? Is it similar to a love filter? –Sevange asked.

"I see that you have experienced it!" said the black lady, amused, looking at each of them, who in turn tried to look away.
–Well, dear ones, at that time it was said that the magician Cagliostro gathered all the ingredients to make the mythical perfume, but some flowers and plants were native to America and for that reason he went to the colonies of New Spain, although the real reason was that he was Marie Antoinette's lover, and his head was in danger like hers, in those circumstances the best thing was to put an ocean in the middle, specifically a place called New Orleans. And after a short time it is said that he managed to make the magical fragrance .
In those distant lands lived an English Botanical witch called Lavender Lavernia was from the Celtic tradition, she and I were great friends, she was married to the viceroy of New Spain Reinaldo de Guzman, one day a party was held in a large mansion of a rich man landowner and at that moment Lavanda and Cagliostro met, although I should better say that

they both secretly recognized each other by the fragrances that their bodies gave off, you should know that at that time any
mention of witchcraft ended at the stake, and yet the Alchemists, everyone adored them when we were basically the same, them and us. It's unfair!

And now my dear Family, let's go to America together! -The black lady shouted with great enthusiasm.

"Wait, what can you tell us about the Golden Skulls Order?" Simon asked.

-Yes of course! Those damned inquisitors and witch hunters have been our enemies for hundreds of years. How is it possible that the Perfumed Society has not informed you about them? Are you hiding something from me?

Simon, Sevange and Estela looked at each other strangely. The Black Lady looked at them with distrust, at that moment Estela took the initiative.

–Excuse our ignorance, but we know very little about that order of witch criminals, the person who informed us was my grandmother, a forest witch, and you already know what those women are like.

–Do you mean that the Aroma Archive is a forest witch? In my time those things didn't happen, now I understand many things.

Everything in its time, my dears, now we go to meet the Botanical Witch of New Orleans.

"Wait, we've gotten the information we're looking for, now it's time to go home," Sevange said upset.

–We can't return without the Angel Crimesi, we have a criminal organization that persecutes us because they believe we have him – Estela argued.

–You are crazy! You cannot go to the past from Limbo or purgatory, nothing like this has ever been done, it is very dangerous, we can get lost in the unknown forever and never return - Sevange shouted.

-Speak clearly! "You're scared and you don't want to come with us," Estela shouted.

-Of course! I love doing a "flight" from limbo to the past with a crazy witch, a murderous dead witch and a drunken witch – explained Sevange, moving his hands with great nervousness.

–At least he referred to me in masculine terms –Simon commented.

–How bad this woman has! -Estela protested.

The black lady took Sevange by the hand and took her to the other end of the room, affectionately caressing her face with her hand.

–Sevange, Sevange, do not be afraid, dear, the blood of an angel and a witch runs through your veins, I guess that you are the Arcanum of strength in the tarot cards on your day

of birth. Therefore you are a fighting and brave woman, the person who protects us, but you have to know that sometimes the feet of a botanical witch do not touch the ground and I know that it is difficult to have nothing to cling to, but trust in us. It is the secret of our strength and determination.

Sevange nodded and returned to the others.

–What did the black lady tell you? -Simon asked.

–That I have confidence in myself. What a woman! He has that "Duende" that would convince me of anything.

–Álora, my dears, come with me to my garden, we have to make the perfume of the vicereine Lavender

Lavernia, you can take the fragrances you need, remember that we are going to war.

The three followed the Black Lady who crossed the room, opened a door and entered a greenhouse full of flowers and plants and a bottle of numerous perfumes and essential oils. Simon and Estela turned their heads back and saw that the previous room they left behind was disappearing, losing its visual clarity, Estela made a sign with her fingers on her lips so that she would not say anything to Sevange.

–The ingredients are Serpentaria, serpol thyme, elemi and buglosse, and of course centaurea, do any of you have jojoba oil? I see from your faces that no, my daughters, you have a long way to go.

They all looked at each other, the black lady's words hid an intention, she wanted to know what level of witchcraft they

had, they assumed that this dangerous woman already knew, they were amateurs nothing like their grandmothers.

–How do you know the perfume of the woman we are going to look for? That's something very personal. Witch's secret! –Sevange asked.

–Lavanda and I were good friends. We were both city botanical witches. We had the same ambitions, but different interests.

My friend pursued wealth and power, I pursued beauty and youth, and in that way we helped each other beat the clock.

–Which birth card corresponds to your friend?

He did not finish the last word of the sentence and Estela was already sorry for the clumsiness committed (the Black Lady had mentioned the ingredients moments before and that already indicated the Tarot card that corresponded to her).

"Estela, bring me that bottle of oil," the Black Lady asked while smiling.

–The last card of the Tarot corresponds to you; The World, its perfume is very powerful is society, sensual, creative, wild, expansive and stormy, Lavender is the "anima mundi."

–Why is its fragrance so powerful? -Simon asked.

–The Arcana of the tarot that are represented by naked women symbolize feminine strength, there is no greater power of creation in the universe like the

Arcana of the World and the Star – Sevange advanced in response.

A sad smile appeared on the hostess's face that did not go unnoticed by Simon, his grandmother smiled the same.

–Well dears! It's finished! Now you should change your clothes, the one you're wearing is too short, and it's possible

that your pretty legs will end up stepping on stacked wood very much...
She opened a chest and took out several dresses and some men's clothing.

–Once again I have to dress in clothes that are not mine, this is becoming a habit, these dresses are suffocating – Estela complained, annoyed.

–Now that we are beautiful and elegant, it is time to spread the fragrance of the Arcanum "the World" through our bodies and hold hands. Remember, let the aroma invade your being, I will concentrate on the Lavender Vicereine and we will fly to meet her.

The four of them stand hand in hand around a small table with the Final Arcanum card in the center of the table.

Chapter 6

THE BOTANY WITCH OF NEW ORLEANS

A soft breeze seemed to surround them while it shook their hair, a distant sound could be heard, despite having their eyes closed they noticed changes in luminosity in the room and in a short period of time everything

disappeared, when they opened their eyes they were lying on the wet ground of a swampy place.

"Please don't let it rain, that's what usually happens in the movies," Estela begged.

"We have landed softly, Estela learns," Sevange told her as a challenge.

–Well, come with me because I have been here before, I advise you to keep your eyes wide open, the Alligators like Witch meat –Lady laughed.

They walked a long distance in silence, the warning from the beautiful companion had had a paranoid effect, they kept looking at both sides of the road, Simon had the gun in his hand.

–There is the house of the landowner Diego Domingo de Ribera, and this is the night where Lavanda and Cagliostro met. I preferred to make the trip at its beginning and because of the decorated lights the party has begun.

A few minutes later, the two doormen dressed in finery arrived at the entrance to the mansion, one on each side of the door, and the soldiers present there prevented them from entering by crossing their arms.

– Bonne nuit soldiers, we are the guests of the Vicereina, go look for her.

The soldier at the entrance nodded to a companion of his and ordered him to go look for her, while they remained at the entrance.

Moments later, a woman came running, holding her dress in her hands, and merged into a hug with the Black Lady. It was the Vicereine of New Orleans, the Botanical Witch Lavender Lavernia, of medium height, she had red hair and big gray eyes. Her face had the paleness of a British woman. Her appearance was elegant due to her social position, although she exuded joviality and freshness typical of a young woman and as beautiful as the black lady. It was not surprising that the two were friends. She had a strange aura. of unit.

Vangeli! Dear, I'm glad to see you, you look so good, I haven't heard from you in a while. You're staying with me! we are going to have fun.
Simon looked at his traveling companions perplexed, no one ever told him the name of the Black Lady.
–I have come to visit you with my friends Botánicas Estela, Sevange and Simon.
–A man? Is he an Alchemist?
–No, he is a relative of mine.
-Interesting! Since when are there Botanical men?
–It's a bit long to explain, tell me Lavender, what are these soldiers doing here?
–It is my personal guard, I have to take precautions, I have been informed of the coming of witch hunters and
inquisitors, so after the party you come with me so that you are safe. I'm glad you decided to visit me.
–I was bored to death at home and I told myself I'm going to visit my beloved Lavender.

–My mother! What a black mood this woman has –Estela whispered to her friends.
"I hope there's food, I'm starving," Simon commented, at the same time that Sevange nodded.

After walking through a long garden covered with hedges, they climbed some steps and entered the large residence together, where there was a large hall full of very elegant people dancing and small groups of people toasting with champagne, with orchestra music, and tables full of food and drink. Lavender held on to Simon's arm as she chatted with the black lady.

"I heard that your relationship with Saint Germain has cooled," Lavender mentioned.

–We traveled together to Lapland, and these things can happen in such cold places.

–Then it is true that you won the emerald from the angel Luzbel from the warmth of some blankets.

–Eternal youth is irresistible dear! -the two friends laughed.

Estela and Sevange looked at each other surprised because the legend was known in another way, since they were

children they had heard that the emerald of youth was a donation from Count Saint Germain to the Perfumed Society.

–How stupid we Witches are, the more beautiful the stories are, the more credible they seem, when the truth is that the Black Lady stole the emerald from Count Saint Germain, it was not a gift of love, in our world nothing is given away... -Estela reflected-

"Speak for yourself, you are the idealist, I never believed that love story," Sevange responded.

But that didn't matter now, they were hungry and approached the tables full of select food.

Lavender walked arm in arm with Simon towards a group of influential people who were authorities of the city, such as politicians, bankers and important personalities, while the Black Lady looked at all the possible exits of doors, windows, stairs, at the same time she was observed by Sevange and Estela while they were eating.

–Have you seen the attitude of our new friend? "He looks like a caged lion," commented Sevange.

–Remember that we come from the future! "I'm sure the Black Lady knows what will happen in the next few hours or minutes," Estela responded.

"Which of these men will be the alchemist Cagliostro," said Sevange.

–It's that one for sure! He is surrounded by women, and some take his hand and read the lines of his destiny, and I see that they are delighted. His bearing is upright and refined, with a harmonious voice, he is in his early thirties. From here I can smell his perfume! It is a flirt! - Estela laughed.

"He's looking at us, and now he's coming here," Sevange said nervously.

–Good evening Ladies, my name is Cagliostro, nice to meet you.

–My name is Estela and this is Sevange, Cagliostro? It is Italian, Slavic, Greek.

–It's a name and little more than what you see! And you? You are not sisters, Hispanic and half-Asian and yet you have the same fragrance.

–What corresponds to the Arcanum! You tell me –Sevange told him, covering Estela's mouth with his hand.

-The world! of course, although I deduce that it is a borrowed fragrance. I could show you my garden with scents to choose from.

Sevange and Estela were speechless, that man's language was captivating, at that moment they realized that they were holding hands, immediately withdrawing it. The scene did not go unnoticed by the black lady who was in a secluded and discreet place, something was not going well, her traveling companions had altered the natural order of things that had happened some time ago, Lavender had chosen Simon as her companion, while cagliostro was fooling around with the wrong botanical witches, he had to fix the scene appropriate. Determined to redirect the situation, she approached to participate in the lively talk, a decision that surprised the alchemist Cagliostro as soon as he saw her.

–Who's coming here! Vangeli von Hohenheim Levy! better known as the Black Lady. What a surprise! "I didn't expect to find you in the colonies, when your preferences are expensive European perfumes," said Cagliostro.

–New fragrances, new packaging, dear, like the one you have hanging on your shoulder: Reindeer Skin? Que tempo quelli!

The Black Lady's observation aroused fear in Cagliostro who held the rope sewn to the elongated leather bag that hung from his shoulder tighter.

–I see that you remember the time spent with the teacher in snowy lands, although the same seduction did not work in such humid and warm lands –Cagliostro said.

–Everything in its time! Heat, humidity and pleasure go together, dear alchemist.

At one end of the room, the Vicereine Lavanda Lavernia, while speaking with the personalities of the city, did not lose sight of the movements of the Black Lady and looked where she focused her eyes, she knew that her friend's visit was not accidental, and the man I bet the guy who was talking to her was wearing something hanging on her back that captivated her attention, because before being a woman of high society, she was a botanical witch, so she decided to join the entourage along with Simón.

–Vangeli dear! You introduce me to your attractive friend - at the same time he made a sign to the servant who was carrying a tray of champagne glasses who served them all -

–With great pleasure, I present to you Mr. Cagliostro, doctor in botanical science, alchemist and conqueror of feminine aromas, as you can see.

Pointing with his hand to Sevange and Estela who were like statues looking at the man in front of them, and to

other women who were a few meters further back who were making signs with their hands.

–Sevange, you understand something about what they are talking about, it seems like a friendly dialogue and yet he throws barbs like daggers –said Estela.

–I think I understand that between them and Count Saint Germain there is a history of jealousy, betrayal and a certain

stolen perfume, all of this spoken in a very subtle way - commented Sevange.

"Look at them, they keep looking at the Cagliostro leather container," Simon commented in a low voice in the ears of his friends, who nodded in agreement.

"I think I guess what it contains," Sevange didn't finish the sentence.

When suddenly shots were heard coming from outside the mansion. Some men approached the vicereine and whispered something in her ear, which changed Lavender's expression.

–Come quickly through that quick hallway! My spies tell me that they are attacking us.

At that moment, several men on horseback with their swords raised, accompanied by rebels for the independence of the colonies, entered the room. In a matter of seconds, blood ran across the elegant floor of the room. The guests tried to defend themselves, but they died. one after another, the soldiers of the vicereine's guard could barely contain the attack, the rebels were very numerous. Simon had taken out his pistol to repel the aggression but the Black Lady prevented him.

–No Simon, this is not our fight. Now run! -shout.

They left the mansion through a door behind a gallery where the stables were, they engaged in a fight with a group of men with their faces covered with a scarf. Sevange surprised everyone with a recital of blows, Simon hit the head with his pistol, The Black Lady was an expert thrower of knives that hit their targets, Cagliostro came with the horses that he had untied from the floats and in a few seconds all of them were on the backs of the animals, except Simon who had to be picked up by the Black Lady. since he didn't know how to ride.

–Come on, follow me, those wretches are coming for us, I wonder how they know our whereabouts? –Virqueen Lavender wondered.They galloped away, pursued by those who had assaulted the mansion, their pursuers were from the order of the Golden Skulls.

They were a very large group of horsemen at the head and behind them were two floats attached to the pursuing group where the inquisitor, their chief, Fray Mateo de Azuaga, was accommodated. Without a doubt the operation was important, a detail that did not go unnoticed by Lavanda Lavernia as she escaped.

–This path takes us to the swamps, we will cross the bridge. Vangeli you already know what you have to do! -Screamed Vicereine Lavender.

When they crossed the wooden bridge, the Black Lady and Simon got off the horse, placed two explosive liquid containers in the middle of the bridge on its side, each hid at one end of the exit, while the others continued riding, minutes later. The chasing group arrived, the black lady took her gun out of her bag as did Simon.

When the pursuing horsemen had made it halfway the Black Lady gave the signal.

-Now!

The two fired the explosive that destroyed a section of the bridge as the horses passed by and fell into the Mississippi River. All the riders fell into the river except for the floats that stopped in time.

"I hope the horses haven't been hurt," Simon commented worriedly.

–Mondie, it is the first time that in my lineage there is a sensitive witch who is also a man "la vita ha le sue surprese."

The two got on their mount, and rode a kilometer where the others were waiting.

–Those explosions are your thing, right Vangeli? –Estela asked.

–I have had the help of Simon, and I am glad that you call me by my name, so much discourtesy bothered me.

–The milk! "That woman is impressive," Simón commented to his friends.

Vicereine Lavender Lavernia spoke and led the march.

–We have gained time, we will go to my mansion there we will be safe, I have a detachment of soldiers that will protect us from any attack but I doubt they will try.

They got back on their horses and rode toward the mansion of Viceroy Reinaldo de Guzman y Acevedo, Lavanda's husband.

An hour later they arrived at the gardens of the viceroy's palace. Strangely alone, one of the servants went out to meet the newly arrived horsemen.

–Hello Zarita, where is everyone? My husband is at home?

–No, madam, your excellency marched yesterday with the entire garrison, a revolt had to be quelled in the city of Baton Rouge, madame vicereine.

–And the rest of the domestic staff?

"The servants went to town to get supplies, my lady," Zarita responded.

Lavender looked at Vangeli with a worried face, and entered the house.

–What's happening, and those faces? -Estela asked.

"Well, we're screwed, we have no one to defend us," Simon responded.

They all entered the large mansion, the maid served drinks and trays with pastries and sweet cookies, while they let themselves fall tiredly on the armchairs and couches. The black lady broke the silence.

–So what do we do now Lavender –asked the Black Lady.

–For now, I will spend the night here in my palace, I still have some loyal men who guard the entrances to the house, although tonight we will not suffer any attacks, with the bridge destroyed they will not be able to get here. I am very sorry for this situation. I told my stupid husband that

the inquisitors were behind the rebel plot, I have my spies for a reason, but he didn't believe me and now I fear the worst.

"Now it is midnight on Saturday, which means we have a day's advantage. Our attackers will respect Sunday, Lord's Day, remember that they are inquisitors," the Black Lady argued.

-Well, what are we waiting for, let's run away, I don't want to know anything about those wild extremists -Cagliostro advanced towards the exit door but no one supported his idea.

–Dear alchemist, it is very dangerous to ride through the swamps at night, you could get stuck in muddy waters at the mercy of alligators, and it is also a good time exchange

knowledge and fragrances – Lavender told him with a smile.

To which he responded with a bow. Cagliostro was the type of man who knew how to navigate any situation, no matter how difficult and dangerous it was, without losing his composure, his gestures were always accompanied by a smile.

"Delighted to serve your grace, my lady," Cagliostro replied.

Sevange and Estela looked at each other and smiled, they concluded that Simon had lost his dance partner.

"Now is a good time for you to explain to us who tonight's attackers are," Simon commented.

"We want to know what we are facing," Sevange added, looking at Vicereine Lavernia.

-OK! In a time gone by a few centuries ago, a group of nine European monks from different religious orders decided to join together to appropriate all the sacred relics that ran around the world. They coveted the power they contained, but it did not take them long to realize their mistake they stored so much wood from the cross of Golgotha that they could build a barn to store several

tons of seeds, the same thing happened with the chalice of the last supper, the famous Grail, they had so many that they could fill several chests with them, as did the famous medal of Saint Bartholomew. The result of all that was the failure of their mission every time. the relics were fake.

One day in France in the Abbey of Cluny all of them had a violent discussion, they debated whether to abandon the holy mission of gathering the sacred relics or turn their eyes towards the witches and appropriate their powers and spells inherited from the angel of the beautiful light (Luzbell).). It so happened that three of the monks in the

group were inquisitors and they were the ones who supported the last option, one night while

Those who wanted to continue the mission of gathering sacred relics were having dinner and died of chicken indigestion.

"How is it possible that someone can die from chicken indigestion," Simon commented in a low voice.

"It's a way of saying they were poisoned," Sevange said quietly.

-Sometime later they associated with the witch hunters and created the Golden Skulls order and now they are here conspiring with the rebels against the viceroy my

husband, they want to catch me and now with greater determination because they know that a famous alchemist is with us with a valuable case.

Today our worst enemy is a monk of the Dominican order, Fray Mateo de Azuaga y Osorio, major inquisitor of the colonies of New Spain. "If anyone of you wants to leave because he is oblivious to all this, I will understand," Lavender Lavernia finished her story.

–When you told me to stay with you that we were going to have fun, did you mean this? -everyone laughed.

We stay with you cheri, we witches protect each other. Right girls! and now take that one out

"French champagne for big occasions, dear," the black lady proposed.

Vicereine Lavender glanced at her maid and with a bow of her head, she took charge of the expressed order and in a few minutes she returned with the foamy drink, serving each of the guests. Simón and Sevange were checking their firearms; they had used up ammunition in the previous "flight" to the insane asylum and vampires.

–Lavender, let me enter your laboratory-garden, I have to make fragrances that make boom –the Black Lady requested.

–Of course dear, the more weapons the better, my servant will show you the way.

-I'm exhausted, I've never had a day like today in my life, if someone could tell me where there is a room for me I would be very grateful - Estela begged.

Sevange and Simon nodded.

-Of course! Zarita will take you to the chambers.

The maid made a gesture with her hands for them to follow her through some corridors of the house until they reached some stairs that led to the first floor of the palace. Once upstairs, she opened a room-living room with several large beds.

–Yes, the gentleman is with me, I will show him his room.

–Thank you, but right now I will stay here to talk to my friends, if you tell me where my room is that will be enough.

–Yes sir, your room is at the end of the corridor, good night.

The maid closed the door behind her, while Sevange and Estela undressed.

–Well, I wanted to talk to you, you have seen how Lavender and the black lady looked at the bag hanging on Cagliostro's shoulder, they looked like two tigers fixing their gaze on their prey, I think the "Crimson Angel" perfume is in the alchemist's bag. leather, Sevange wanted to tell us something about the packaging – Simon commented.

-Yeah! The bag is made of reindeer skin, an animal native to Lapland, its body is bathed by the northern lights, due to this peculiarity its skin is an excellent protector for the conservation of magical scrolls from ancient times, for

example "The Lucis spell" it was said that It was written by an angel, hence the interest of those two women in the alchemist Cagliostro. And now someone explain to me what the three of us are doing in the same bed, for example the expert in amorous perfumes –said the surprised Sevange.

–Well yes, you will see the fragrance that we use in the church by mistake, it is a Venetian love filter that penetrates deeply into the skin and has an immediate effect, although the duration is shorter by about two years –said Estela with a broken voice while He caressed Sevange's face.

-two years! –Sevange said surprised, looking at Simon.

–There are other filters with slower effects, but they last ten or twenty years, we have still been lucky –said Estela, relieved.

–You mean that I will have two girlfriends for two years.

–Is this a problem for you? -Sevange asked.

– No, of course not, in fact when I was a child I always wanted to have a witch girlfriend, and I think that both forest witches and city witches are equally crazy, and that's how the women I like are.

–Well now you have both – declared Sevange and after a few seconds of silence the three burst into laughter.

Meanwhile, on the other side of the mansion, the Black Lady, the dead witch with a languid smile, worked for

several hours in the botanical garden of the Lavender Vicereine, mixing essential oils with alcohol and sulfur.

While he was making his explosives he remembered times gone by when his fragrances were the best in Paris and London had all of Europe at his feet, of Madame Pompadour's jealousy of his perfumes and above all he remembered when his card of destiny was The Star, the most powerful in the world. Tarot. The naked and free feminine energy that flows from the celestial to the terrestrial like a blanket of perfumed water, creator of life and unifying love of men and women in its path, the good Star.

But her war over time, and her rebellion against losing beauty and youth led her into a spiral of betrayal, blood and destruction, now her Arcane card of destiny was the one that had no name. "Death."

In another room of the palace the situation was more relaxed.

–Ufff, my mother, what a loving frenzy, anyone would say that we are in danger –said Estela, resting her hand on her forehead.

–I think we should avoid being near a bed when the three of us are together, much less undress. Is it true that the love filter contains horse semen? -Sevange asked.

"Yes, although you can also use a woman's vaginal secretion, now that I think about it... My grandmother doesn't have horses," Estela suddenly stopped.

- I feared! –Sevange sighed.

–I propose that we dress in those nightgowns that are hanging on that rack, and go investigate where is Cagliostro to know what is inside that saddlebag that he never leaves, it may contain the perfume we are looking for, we have to change our attitude or we will never get out of bed - Simon proposed.

Once dressed and in silence, they quietly left the room and, carrying a lit candle, walked through its innumerable corridors and halls.

– Maybe in the rooms on the ground floor we will find something.

–No Simon, there are the smallest rooms, reserved for service, I know from experience –Estela summarized.

–Look at the end of that small staircase there is a glass area, it must be the botanical laboratory –Sevange assured.

–They went up the steps of the stairs and at the end they walked down a small corridor and crouching in the lower area of the door, which was made of wood and glass at the

top, they saw the black lady immersed in her work and thoughts.

–That woman has been working for hours, when does she plan to go to sleep?

"Remember that Estela is dead," Sevange reminded him.

–Deep down I feel sorry for her, the beautiful lonely Witch. -Simon reasoned sadly.

– My grandmother Crisol explained to me that beauty can be a curse, when men and women turn their faces in astonishment to look at you, dazzled by so much charm, and so year after

year they can upset the most balanced woman, even if she is a city Witch. .

They walked through the other wing of the viceroy's palace when a door perfectly decorated with gold trim caught their attention. They entered it without making noise and crouching down and saw the typical bed from the time of the Sun King of France with columns in the corner covered with a mesh curtain at one end of the immense room, you could see the silhouette of two people, but only one deep breath, luckily near the door there was a large couch, where they could hide, at the same time that a naked woman stood up of the bed, it was Lavender. Lavernia

covered her body with a maroon silk robe. "He has Reindeer's skin bag with him, the other person sleeping must be the alchemist, I don't remember his name," Estela explained in a whisper.

–His name is Cagliostro, he has taken the parchment and has a bottle in his other hand with a quill, now he is looking for something on a table – Sevange commented in a low voice.

–Look for a sheet of paper, the same thing happens to me when I need a sheet I never find it – Estela commented.

Simon made a gesture, putting his index finger to his lips, for silence.

The Vicereina approached a chair where her scarf was hanging, picked it up and spread it on the table.

"Look, he is writing on his scarf the magical spells and incantations from the parchment "The Lucis Spell." He is copying it," Sevange said in astonishment.

–Haven't you noticed a strange fragrance? -said Estela.

–The unknown fragrance that we have perceived may be the Crimson Angel perfume that we are looking for and that Cagliostro manufactured had it next to the parchment, in a very old alabaster bottle – explained Sevange.

They were waiting for a long period of time until the Vicereine finished writing and left the room towards her botanical laboratory where the Black Lady was.

Moment they took advantage of to take the scented alabaster jar and leave the bag with the parchment in its place and stealthily leave the room.

"Simon, you're very quiet, it's obvious that you like that woman. I hope you don't sleep with a gun under your nightgown," Estela commented, laughing.

Men! -Sevange said, shaking his head.

Suddenly they heard a terrifying scream that frightened them so much that they dropped the small lamp to the ground.

–Damn what was that! -Simon asked upset.

"The scream was coming from the direction of that dark corridor," Sevange indicated.

Estela and Sevange looked at Simón, pleading with their eyes to return to the room and forget about the subject.

–In any circumstance I am a police officer.

Simon walked forward in the indicated direction and they followed him.

-Perfect! "We are going to meet danger in our nightgown and with a candle in our hands," Estela replied reluctantly.

They reached the end of the hallway where a wall prevented them from continuing, they turned left and saw that the floor made a descent that ended in a half-open iron door.

Simon, why are you stopping, what's worrying you? -Sevange asked.

–Open doors are an invitation to danger, every police officer knows that, stand behind me.

They crossed the threshold of the door and walked through numerous galleries that intersected each other, the walls were made of unworked rock stone like a cave can be, the

floor was sand, they understood that they were in the basement of the viceroy's house.

–This labyrinthine place looks like an old mine, what's the point of something like that in a palace, I would understand if it were a cellar or a basement but this? -Sevange commented worried.

At that moment Estela tripped over something that made her fall to the ground on top of something soft. When Simon brought the candle to the ground, Estela saw that her face was a few centimeters away from the open eyes of a woman with a

shattered head and completely dead. moment when he unleashed a scream of terror that resonated throughout the underground, causing a sinister echo.

rising with an impulse that she herself did not know she possessed.

–She's a dead woman, Simon! -Screamed Estela scared.

Sevange moved the lamp in a circle and the light made several corpses appear scattered on the floor, all of them women. Simon crouched down to examine them.

– These poor women have their bodies destroyed, it is as if a wild animal had torn them to pieces.

–They all dress the same way as if they were uniformed –Sevange asked himself.

"They are the maids of the viceroy's mansion, so they didn't go to town for supplies," Estela concluded, looking at Sevange and Simon.

–And due to the rigidity of their bodies, they have been dead for at least a day, which means that the scream we

heard did not come from them. This is getting very ugly girls, it's a trap! Suddenly a roar was heard and a monstrous bipedal being, two meters high, with legs of a goat, the face of a lion and the claws of a bear, came running from one of the galleries and jumped on top of Simon and when he tried to stick his paw in Sevange hit him on the head with the lamp, which made the beast retreat and buy a few seconds so he could look for

something to defend himself with, but an hour ago they had gotten out of bed and were only wearing a white nightgown. on top of a naked body.

When the beast was going to charge in a second attack, Lavender and Vangeli opportunely appeared, firing their weapons. They were pistols that only allowed a single shot (one of them hit the monster's head), although it was enough to make the beast bend its knees shortly after.

Black Lady threw a vial of fluid at him that surrounded him like a transparent bluish bubble.

–In a few minutes he will run out of air and this monster brought from the astral depths will die – explained the Black Lady.

–How is it possible that a chimera-animal lived under my house? I ordered this place to be built as an escape route, a

back door for a botanical witch – Lavender explained as she looked at the corpses.

–Because we are not the only witches here, right Zarita!

From the shadows appeared the figure of a woman with a gun in each hand.

–That's right, I am the witch of the swamps and in New Orleans there is no place for two witches, much less a foreign one. As you have discovered me!

"You said that the maids went to town to buy groceries, but the wagon was in the stables. And because like is always recognizable," said the Black Lady.

–Damn murderous black witch! why have you killed these poor women? -Virqueen Lavender reproached.

–They suspected me and could ruin my plans to own this mansion worthy of a powerful witch like me.

–Now I understand, it was you who reported me to the inquisition and that is why they knew that I was at the celebration of the landowner Diego de Ribera, and tonight you drugged Cagliostro –Lavanda protested.

"Yes, I will hand over the alchemist as was the deal, but with you I have the license to kill you," Zarita threatened.

The swamp witch was about to open fire when fortunately Cagliostro appeared from behind, staggering, hitting Zarita's head with a stone, at which point the Black Lady

took the opportunity to throw a knife that stuck in the neck of the murderous witch, collapsing into the ground. floor, falling on top of the dead chimeric monstrous creature.

-My God! "It's more dangerous to live here than in France," exclaimed Cagliostro, looking at the ground dizzily, while trying to keep his balance.

"And if that were not necessary, we have the presence of ghosts," he exclaimed, looking at Simon, Estela and Sevange who were dressed in white nightgowns from the darkness of the gallery.

–Very timely, your alchemist assistance has saved us from this crazy criminal, I hope that in the future you don't fall asleep so soon –Lavender thanked.

"Well, now Lavender and I won't take care of all this, it will soon be dawn, you can retire to your rooms, Simon with you," ordered the Black Lady.

"I can stay to help you," Simon offered.

But Sevange and Estela took him arm in arm and walked in silence through the galleries until they found the exit door.

Once outside the sinister place they reached the hallways of the rooms and after a long time without saying a word.

–The...The next time I have a romantic encounter I stay in bed relaxed until the next day, damn it! -said Estela moving her index finger up and down, Sevange and Simon nodded their heads.

–We have obtained the perfume of power "the crimson angel" now we are each going to sleep in our own bed and tomorrow we will return home – said Sevange, relieved.

Chapter 7
THE FOULAR OF THE VIRREINA.

The next day in the middle of the afternoon, one by one, except for Lavanda and Cagliostro, they appeared in the main room, impatience reigned in the atmosphere.

–Everything has gone according to plan, the Vicereina and the alchemist have met, and now that they are sleeping it is the ideal time to go home – Estela proposed.

–No, we all have to continue together and stay united, the Golden Skulls are after us, if they catch us they will torture us and we will surely end up at the stake – answered the Black Lady.

–Well said Vangeli! I propose to go to the city of Baton Rouge, we have a Spanish military barracks and my husband the Viceroy is there gathering the troops, there we will be safe from those damned murderers - Lavender

commented, appearing perfectly dressed and groomed to ride.

–Where is Cagliostro? -asked the Black Lady.

-Who knows! When I woke up he wasn't in the room, that's how these men are, they appear and disappear like a night fog.

Yesterday he told me about going up the Mississippi in a boat, anyway! -Lavender said.

When they left the house they went to the stable and brought the horses with their saddles ready to ride, all of them were ready to leave except Simon who did not know how to ride a horse.

But fate had another plan prepared for him: a huge fire could be seen on the horizon. The faces of discouragement

and regret appeared on all of them, they could not escape, they were trapped.

Those damn murderers! They have set fire to the roads, they want to corner us like rats. What do we do, Lavender? -Sevange asked alarmed- "Well, the three of us have nothing to do with a colonial war and independence, perhaps it's time to go to our little house," said Estela, shaking hands.

–If we Botanical witches are captured, you will have no future to return to nor a little house to go to, dear Estela, –inquired the Vicereine.

"You mean that what happens here will have an impact on our lives in the future," Simon recited, alarmed, looking at the fire on the horizon. Estela looked at the Black Lady and she confirmed, nodding, the words that the Vicereine said a moment before.

–Lavanda knows that we have made a flight from the future. We all carry her fragrance and that is something that does not go unnoticed by a witch - revealed the Black Lady.

–Okay, what's the plan? "We are ready to fight until the end," Sevange said determinedly.

"They will try to assault the Viceroy's mansion by crossing the labyrinthine garden, Estela and I will place explosives at the entrance," the Black Lady proposed.

–The rest of us will stand at the exit of the garden with the horses prepared to flee-Lavender announced next.

Shortly after, a detachment of rebel troops for independence approached a short distance from the mansion, remaining stationed.
The Black Lady and Estela placed the containers of explosive botany in strategic places at the entrance to the garden of the Viceroy's mansion.
–There they are, I didn't think they were so numerous, aren't you afraid Vangeli?
–It's nothing compared to other situations I've experienced, like escaping from an inquisition dungeon in France. Those smells of clogged latrines, of rotting fungi, of sweat and blood on the walls even made the rats sick, it was terrifying and yet I was able to escape being burned in a courtyard full of screaming people. And here we are dear.
–I'm sorry that one of my ancestors killed you, really!
–Throughout life we die many times, in one way or another, it will happen to you too*
–It was said about you that you were bisexual. Was it true?
–Dear, we botanical witches do not need labels, we love, we hate or we are indifferent, and when we go beyond two hundred years of life we prefer the latter....- The Lady stopped talking, suddenly she realized that her shoes were stepping on something watery, it was blood. .

–They are the soldiers of the viceroy who were guarding, they are dead.- Estela shouted in alarm.
Suddenly a group of men came out from behind some hedges, they were advancing towards them firing their weapons, they were the witch hunters.
–Run away Estela! "I will face them," the Black Lady shouted while shooting with a pistol in each hand, exploding the explosives.
A large number of armed men jumped into the air to fall dead to the ground, some collided with the wall that surrounds the garden, but the shot of one of the hunters hit Estela, falling to the ground, the Black Lady rushed to help Estela. He stood in the line of fire of the hunter who was preparing to finish off the woman who was on the ground.

They both fired their weapons, they looked into each other's eyes for a time that seemed like an eternity and they both fell to the ground, mortally wounded.

Moments later, Simon, Sevange and Lavanda arrived to repel the attack, the rest of the attackers fled on horseback at a gallop.

Simon lifted Estela's body with his arms, while Sevange tried to clean the wound with oil that was located under the collarbone.

"Let's go to the mansion, there, we'll be safe," Simon shouted.

The Lavender Vicereine slowly approached the body that was lying on the ground of her beloved Black Lady, she fell to her knees....

– Mom, Mom! –Lavender murmured tearfully.

The others were shocked by the Vicereine's statement.

–We didn't know that the lady...Vangeli was your mother –said Sevange.

–Witch's secret! –Lavender murmured in a low voice as she rested her head on her mother's body.

The moment was one of immense sadness, to protect themselves the witches had to keep the family relationship a secret with the pain that this entails for the witch who

was going to die. It was known from the spoken chronicles the desires of the Black Lady to have a family. .

Lavender took the tarot card the Arcanum of "the Star" from her pocket and placed it on the chest of the beautiful witch Vangeli while she held her hand and pronounced the phrase known to witches in her mother's ear.

–Forget, dream, everything begins again.

At that moment the Black Lady opened her eyes and spoke her last words.

––Death has touched me by lot and I return to the starting box, da capo fine (from beginning to end) –and he breathed his last.

And instantly something beautiful and unexpected happened, the body of the black lady was illuminated by a powerful light that ascended towards the sky and then disappeared.

–What happened Simon? You are the sensitive one. Can you guess what has happened? –Lavender asked him.

–Your mother's gesture saving Estela's life has redeemed her from her past and has recovered her birth fragrance, the good star. It is what she wanted, to recover Angel's magic and be the botanical witch that she once was, teacher of the Perfumed Society.

I think in the end he wanted to save all of us.

–Thank you Simon! We are family but I don't know what to call you, how strange it is all true - Lavender said with tears in her eyes.

"That's our world, weird as hell," Simon said with a half smile.

Simón and Sevange walked in the direction of the Viceroy's palace. Sevange turned his head and...

–Lavender, you should get safe and come in with us.

The vicereine shook her head affirmatively and everyone together passed through the gate of the mansion.

Once inside, they placed Estela's body on a couch with the intention of extracting the bullet.

–Take Belladonna oil mixed with amarita, it will numb you, so you will not feel pain.

–No, our friend is a Forest Witch, she is too emotional for that concoction, she could be touched in the head.

–We have to take the risk Sevange, if I can't extract the bullet it won't make it through tonight – Simón assured – wake up Estela, drink this medicine, it will relieve your

pain – in seconds she opened her eyes and obeyed the suggestion.

–Tell me Simon! When did you decide to be a botanical witch? –Estela
asked.

–Why do you want to know?

–Well, we have "flew" to the past together, we have lain in bed, now you
are healing my wound, Damn!!

Simon swallowed...

–I think it was when I was a child, at first I wanted to be a police
officer like my grandfather, but one autumn afternoon my mother and
my aunt took me to the cinema to see Snow White and the Seven
Dwarfs, I suppose they wanted to show me how evil and diabolical
witches are and dissuade me. to continue with the family tradition but
they achieved the opposite effect, what child likes a girl who sings and
dances with the birds, in reality I was fascinated by the beautiful witch
and finally when I was older I became a "perfumed" police officer. And
now Here I am in the company of some

incredible women trapped in a military fort-palace in the eighteenth
century.

Estela lost consciousness again.

–The bullet is in a very difficult position to extract, only a doctor with
surgical instruments can do it.

"We have to go home quickly," Sevange said quickly, "but how?" With
Estela passed out we cannot return.

–If we surrender we will be treated as political prisoners, since it is a war
for independence

and Estela may be taken to the hospital.

–No Simon, there is much more at stake here, out there surrounding us
are witch hunters and an order of fanatical

inquisitors eager for power. When they get what they want, what do
you think they'll do with me? witch, Jew and British, in a few minutes
my fragrance will be like roasted meat, and you will suffer the same fate.

Sevange and Simon looked at each other disheartened, the Vicereine's arguments were by far the most likely thing to happen.

Suddenly, outside the walls of the house, voices were heard inviting the vicereine to be seen.

–Well, let's go to parley with those traitors.

The vicereine, together with Sevange and Simon, carrying Estela in her arms, climbed some stairs that ended on the

terrace of the viceroy's palace, ready to talk with the assailants.

Below in the palace gardens were stationed the rebel forces of Captain Avellaneda, accompanied by Monsignor Fray Mateo de Azuaga y Osorio, along with him several hooded monks with

black cassocks that guarded the alchemist Cagliostro.

–They have the alchemist prisoner, you said Lavender left on her own, how is it possible that he is here? -Simon asked.

They looked at the vicereine waiting for a response.

–It was our escape plan for all of us on a boat down the Mississippi River, in case things looked bad, as you know we witches always have a back door.

–Greetings, my lady viceroy, I regret that we have to talk in these strange circumstances and above all, I regret the loss of your husband, Viceroy Reynaldo de Guzman, from the Spanish crown.

–Greetings Monsignor Azuaga y Osorio and to you Captain Avellaneda, as vicereine of New Orleans. He ordered them to lay down their weapons and abandon their plans to raid my house.

–I am afraid that this is not possible, my lady, we will take the Viceroy's palace and everyone in it will be taken prisoner. Our flag for

The liberation of New Orleans will wave again –the captain threatened.

–In that case we have nothing more to talk about, we will fight until the end –concluded Vicereine Lavender.

–Wait, my vicereine!! We are educated and peaceful people, send us what is ours and belongs to the alchemist Cagliostro. - pleaded the monk Fray Azuaga, head of the Golden Skull order -

"That damned Dominican monk ate at our table, I never liked him, I distrusted him, I told my husband and now he's dead," Lavender murmured to Simon.

"My lady, we do not intend to cause you any harm, we only intend to recover what is mine," Cagliostro demanded.

–Sevange and Simon looked at each other in surprise. The vicereine had deceived them. There was no escape plan. The alchemist joined the order of the Golden Skull to save his life.

–What is happening Lavender! The alchemist has betrayed us - Sevange shouted - and you have deceived us, there is no escape plan.

–If it exists, come with me Simon.

They walked through a passage after moving a candelabra that was attached to a wall that moved, revealing a path to follow.

–Dear Simon, take this route, it ends in the underground basement where last night we had an unfortunate adventure, continue in the same direction and you will come out along a rural road far from here and the swamps.

–You're not coming with us? You will die if you stay here.

–I have pending accounts to settle, dear little brother. Tell me something, Simon. Which of those two women is your fiancée or lover?

–We are a couple of three.

–A couple of three? Wow! I think I would like to live in Barcelona. So the three of you form a witches' triangle?

-Among other triangles

–As I said, I think I would like Barcelona -They both laughed-

They both returned to the terrace where Sevange was taking care of Estela.

–It's good that you have returned, that horrible noise is because they are trying to break the huge entrance door with axes, we have to get out of here.

–We have a chance to flee and save our lives –said Simon. –Help me lift Estela, I know a way out soon we will be safe –Simon hastened to say. While the Vice Queen Witch of New Orleans Lavender Lavernia began to undress, to the astonishment of Simon and Sevange.

–But what is this woman doing! "It's breaking down," exclaimed Sevange.

———————-

A few hours before, shortly after Estela drank the potion that had been given to her, she entered a dream state outside the body, where she found herself floating through the rooms of the enormous mansion and being an invisible witness to all of their conversations, about how the vicereina and the alchemist Cagliostro hatched a plan that was not about escape, but rather about joining the enemies and attracting them to the Viceroy's Mansion.

How the Black Lady explained to her daughter Lavender the deadly power of the "Crimson Angel"

She actually had no intention of escaping to the city of Baton Rouge to meet with the Viceroy, she knew that her husband was dead.

At that moment, while the vicereine was undressing, Estela opened her eyes.

"It's a trap!" Estela shouted, waking up.

The Vicereine was taking off her clothes, first her dress, then her petticoats, until she was naked, carrying a scarf in her hands as the only garment, while a soft breeze blew.

–The love and revenge of a Renaissance witch begins as a light breeze to end as a storm of blood and horror. "Now, my dears, don't look at me," Lavanda said, looking at her companions on the terrace.

The lavender witch sang as she walked over her naked body the scarf that moved like a snake that had taken on a life of its own, at the same time that she climbed some steps to an atrium where the flagpole was.

From there she could see the army that surrounded her. He watched, fascinated by that sinister deadly dance with the scarf moving over his naked body like an impatient lover.

–Estela took out from one of her pockets a tarot card that corresponds to the final Arcanum "the World" whose

representation is a naked woman dancing with a scarf – at that moment the whole scene became clear to her.

–Where did this strong wind come from? What is happening? –Sevange shouted, grabbing Simon's arm.

–The other night in the vicereine's room we thought we saw that Lavender was writing with a goose quill in her scarf the spells from the parchment "The Lucis Spell" but in reality she used the perfume of the "Crimson Angel" as an inkwell so that both things They are written on the scarf – Estela shouted in the midst of thunderous lightning that illuminated the sky.

–You mean that he changed the alabaster perfume for his own! –Sevange concluded.

–Yes, she knew we were there and she made us see the scene that suited her and then meet with the Black Lady. Don't look at the vicereine or we will die!

The dance of the botanical witch of New Orleans was taking a sinister turn, the skin of her body was turning into an orange tone like the rise of the full moon, her eyes were like burning embers of fire, her gaze was directed at the enemies that They were besieging her and in turn they were petrified watching how that hypnotic and sensual dance was taking over their will and would lead them to death.

–The quiet emotion of first love is born from desire and feeling. I am your lives, I am the world.

"Fight among yourselves until your last breath, you will find no greater happiness than dying for your mistress and mistress of our lands, the botanical vicereine of New Orleans," sang the witch Lavender in a horrible and sinister litany.

–We have to get out of here now! "The curse will reach us," Sevange hastened to say.

But it seemed that Estela and Simon had their gaze motionless, watching the horrible scene that was opening before their eyes.–The rebel soldiers of Captain Avellaneda and the troops of the inquisitor Fray Mateo de Azuaga are fighting each other to the death with swords and firearms,

although they are surrounded by the flames of the torches they do not seem to care much, they are burning and continue fighting until he dies – Simon murmured, impressed – except for the alchemist who used a black blindfold for his eyes.

Captain Avellaneda faced the inquisitor monk in a savage fight with sword and knife, consumed by hatred, their bodies burned in flames, without uttering a single scream, they finally died.

The witch hunters, intoxicated by the beautiful and terrifying dance of the Vicereine, burned themselves naked before the vicereine of New Orleans.

Estela had her hands covering her face so as not to look at such horror.

"And the most horrible thing of all is that they kill and die with a smile of happiness on their faces," said Sevange in a small voice.

–In the underground of the fortress there is a secret passage to leave the fort, it is our salvation, let's go –Simon hastened to say.

They helped Estela get up and ran towards the stairs where the entrance to the basement began but the fire did not allow them to advance, they were surrounded by flames.

"I will try to get you out of here and return home," said Estela determinedly.

– In the end the fire always accompanies us as the witches that we are – Simon ironized.

–Without the Black Lady we cannot return, she brought us here, we need a gateway to our world, to our time –Sevange lamented.

–I hope you make it! Lavender has fled together with the alchemist Cagliostro, while he was consummating his revenge, now his enemies have died, we are alone Estela! "We trust you," said Simon.

"Quickly put on this fragrance and hold hands and don't ask me anything," Estela begged.

Sevange put his face close to Estela's ear and pronounced the words that define the magical triangle they form.

"forget, dream, everything begins again."

Chapter 8

The perfumed society

And instantly they noticed different shades of colors that were forming around them, the wind had stopped blowing. The vicereine and the alchemist had fled.

Silence made its way around their bodies just at the moment when the viceroy's palace was consumed by flames, everything was over, everything was left behind, only the sight of all those dead men reminded them of the terrible tragedy they had experienced moments before. .

And as if they fell from a great height, they landed on top of a large table that broke into a thousand pieces, causing a roar in the séance room, causing all the guests at the session who were around the table holding hands to fall to the ground. ground terrified. They thought that dead people from the past had returned to the world of the living because of the clothes they wore.

–Ahhh, my God, how scary, they almost scared me to death! You guys again! Where have you come from? –Madame Malhues shouted furiously.

"Damn, my back is broken," Simon lamented.

"Sorry, sorry, don't be afraid, we are living people, we dress like this for a fair performance," Estela apologized while Simón and Sevange helped her get up.

–I also brought you a gift, look, isn't it a beautiful perfume?

The medium's furious expression suddenly changed.

-You have remembered! "Tomorrow is my birthday," Madame Malhues proclaimed happily to her frightened guests who had fallen on the floor, crawling on the floor looking for the exit door while they looked at the ceiling with wide eyes wondering where these people had fallen from and with fear embedded in their hearts. body.

"Of course you'll have to pay me for a new table," he said, pointing to the pieces of wood scattered on the floor.

–Naturally dear! and now I'll borrow your car, okay? – Estela said, taking the keys from the shelf.

"Let's get out of here quickly," Estela said quickly as she took Sevange and Simon's hands.

"You have to call a doctor, your wound is bleeding," Sevange said worriedly.

–No, let's not go quickly –and he hurried to get into the car.

"What a perfume you gave it," Simon said worriedly.

--My grandmother's love filter, I'm sure they'll get over the scare.

–Upon hearing this last, Simon and Sevange ran to the car and hurried out of there.

–Come to my party tomorrow, but enter through the door, please! –Madame Malhues shouted from the window.

–Thank you Estela, you were fantastic, it's better not to talk about the flight because my whole body hurts but it saved our lives.

–Simon can't hear you, Estcla has fainted! "Let's go to the hospital quickly," Sevange expressed with concern.

"We will go along the main road and soon we will see traffic signal indicators warning of the proximity of a hospital," said Simon.

And so it happened, a few kilometers later they saw the detour that took them to the general medical center of Ibiza, when they arrived Simon took her in his arms while Sevange went to the counter to call the nurses.

–Quickly take her to the operating room, she has a projectile on the right side below her collarbone, I am a police inspector.

But when he wanted to take it out of his pocket. The police badge saw that he did not have it, he took off his jacket to examine it pocket by pocket but it was not there.

–What's wrong Simon? –Sevange asked.

–I've lost my police badge!

–Well, at least we have saved Estela's life and the doctors will save her. We are going to the cafeteria to have something to eat and then to the waiting room to rest.

Hours later a surgeon tapped Inspector Simon on the shoulder.

waking him up from sleep in one of the armchairs in the waiting room.

-Mister! I'm Dr. Gaban. Your friend is out of danger. We have removed this metal projectile. Right now we are moving her to a room on the third floor. We have given her antibiotics and a strong painkiller so she can sleep all night.

-Thank you very much doctor!

"We will rest in this Sevange room and tomorrow we will go see her," Simon proposed.

–Okay, I'm dead asleep, good night.

–The next morning the sun came through the windows of the waiting room, illuminating Sevange's face, causing him to wake up.

–Simon, wake up! How did you sleep?

–It's not a bed, but I'm glad to be in the twentieth century... Hey, don't cry Sevange, we're home, in the end everything turned out well

well, well, better release all the accumulated tension.

–I have seen terrible things Simon! –Sevange said disconsolately.

Simon hugged Sevange, he understood that he needed to cry and cry, after everything he had recently experienced.

–You have a handkerchief! I don't want Estela to see me crying.

Simon offered him the wide sleeve of his eighteenth-century shirt, which made Sevange laugh. They walked through the hospital to meet

Estela and when they arrived at her room they saw that she was still
sleeping.

–It's mid-morning and she's still asleep, I think it's better that she
recovers here for a few days – Simon replied.
–The "Witch flights" consume a lot of energy from the body and if she
is also injured she will surely be exhausted. It is better to let her sleep.
Tomorrow she will be as good as new, she has the blood of an angel
–Sevange stated.
–I know, she has been very brave for an inexperienced witch, she has
deserved that we let her rest and now it is time to return to Barcelona,
I think I know where they have kidnapped those girls.
–I'm not going anywhere without Estela, much less leaving her alone in
a hospital. You said we were a couple of three.
–And we are, but when he wakes up he will want to come with us even
if he can't stand up, you know the character he has, he is not easy to
convince.
Sevange looked at Estela sleeping through the window in the bedroom
door and recognized that Simón was right.
–Okay, let's go to Barcelona.
They left the hospital heading to the airport but realized that they were
broke and dressed in Renaissance clothing.

–We'll go to the bank where I have a checking account and then we'll stop by a clothing store, is that okay with you? –Simon proposed.

-Perfect! I'm tired of people's looks.

An hour later they were on the plane, after a while of silence Simon realized by looking at Sevange's face that she was worried about Estela.

–Sevange, how did you discover the phrase that defines the three of us?

–I don't know, it just happened Crisol told us that it is something that comes to our aid when we need it, suddenly those words came to me.

–Now tell me, Simon, what do you plan to do when we get to Barcelona? You said you knew where the "Golden Skulls" are hiding.

–I will go to the police headquarters and request a brigade to arrest those guys and free the kidnapped perfumer girls. In the hospital cafeteria I told them by phone that I would need police reinforcements. Shortly after they arrived at the Barcelona airport terminal

When they arrived at passport control, several police officers approached and grabbed Sevange's arms and handcuffed her behind her back.

–Simon, but what are they doing? Tell him you're a police officer.

"Take her into custody, there is an international arrest warrant against her," Simon said as he walked away from the scene.

–Simooooonnn! Damn! You are as stupid as your grandfather - Sevange shouted angrily, who knew the family history.

———————-

While in a hospital room in Ibiza lying in bed, Estela, already awake, remembered everything she experienced in that mythical time of witches in New Orleans, all the misfortunes experienced, the flights from one place to another, all those deaths, nothing nice to remember and despite All of this showed that something was missing to complete that puzzle, but what? As he looked at the walls

around him, he noticed how the bandage covered and pressed on his shoulder. It was clear that he was in a

hospital. But where? He barely remembered anything, it must have been due to the effects of the anesthesia. He pressed the call button on the table next to the bed. In a few minutes the nurse arrived.

–Hello miss, how are you, do you need something.

–If you tell me where I am?

–At the General San Ramón hospital in Ibiza, the doctor visits her tomorrow to see how she is.

–Do you know something about the people who brought me here!

–Yes, they told me that you should stay in the hospital for a few days resting until the doctor discharges you, they went to the airport. By the way, the dress you were wearing is in the laundry room and the perfume bottles you had are in the table drawer

–Well, thank you very much for everything.

The nurse left the room and Estela immersed herself in her thoughts and concluded that her friends were right. She was tired, injured, with a sore body, so a few weeks in the

hospital resting and eating well would be wonderful for her, and she deserved it after what she had experienced. He
had lived through the last few days and all the horrors he had to see. I am a botanical witch of the perfumes of peace and love, damn it! Let them be the ones to finish the job...-a few minutes later while looking at the ceiling of the room.
–Fuck!!
She got out of bed determinedly and went to the closet to get dressed, but there were only men's clothes in the closet.
At that moment he realized that his roommate behind the curtain was a man.
"Well, now I have to dress in these clothes, it seems I have a problem with clothing and it also has a hat," he said in a low voice while adjusting his pants.
Once dressed, she quietly left the hospital without being seen. Luckily, she had some coins in her pants to call a friend to take her to the airport. In a few minutes a car stopped on the sidewalk where she was.
While on the other side of the sea, Inspector Simon Borrull entered the central police station in Barcelona and quickly went to the director general's office, where he rapped his knuckles on the door.

-Mr. Principal! Do you give your permission?
–Borrull man, come in, come in! Where had he gone? you are very emaciated.
–Well, I have been in several skirmishes, while I was investigating some clues that took me to the Balearic Islands. I have discovered where that gang of international criminals is holding the girls hostage.

About two hundred years ago the viceroy of the colonies of New Spain came to Barcelona when the Viceroy of her

husband died, she built a palace in the center of the city, on Las Ramblas. Well, that gang of criminals is looking for an object that the viceroy brought from the colonies.

By the way, Mr. General Director, I lost my badge while fighting with some guys.

The police chief looked at Inspector Simon in disbelief. What is this guy talking about, he thought? two hundred years? Vicereina? He opened a drawer in his table and handed him a police badge.

–Here you go, a provisional. Do you mean that they had those girls kidnapped right under our noses? Have all the agents necessary to put an end to these guys. I'm sure he'll screw up and that way I'll be able to get rid of the "perfumed policeman," the chief commissioner thought.

–Yes sir, today we will finish this matter.

Police inspector Simon Borrull was going to carry out the biggest operation of his life, he was in the garage and while he was checking his weapon the other agents were getting into the police cars but a feeling of emptiness accompanied him, he missed his two friends, he noticed that he had gotten used to facing danger with them, it's not that he didn't trust his fellow police officers but there was something that didn't fit him, if those guys were looking for the Crimson perfume they were in the right place, the vicereine's palace. Why kidnap those girls?

But a fortuitous event tore him from his train of thought, several dark-colored cars blocked the exit of the police parking lot where a group of elegantly suited men got out of

the cars and approached Inspector Borrull who quickly pointed his gun at them.

–Lower your gun, Inspector Borrull, I am the Chief of the provincial police region, Victor Garmendia, here is my documentation.

–Who are those guys? They have blocked our exit, I imagine they are coming with you.

–That's right, inspector, these gentlemen are security personnel from the American embassy in Madrid, and the Minister of the Interior called me this morning to

Ask me to talk to you and demand that you collaborate with them in everything they ask of you, this is a political matter, for now you will come with us and you have to answer some questions.

While they were talking, agent Albert Cusido approached the two of them. The inspector took the opportunity to ask where they were taking him; he wanted his assistant to hear the conversation.

"Let's go to the offices of the American Consulate, there we will discuss some issues," the police chief ordered while looking contemptuously at Agent Cusido.

–Right now we have to rescue some women who remain kidnapped –replied the inspector.

– Other people will take care of that!

–Can I talk to my men? Agent Cusido call the airport police and tell them to release a girl they are holding named Sevange

Visconti on my order, then make a phone call to the Ibiza general hospital and ask about the condition of the patient Estela Portabella.

–Yes, Mr. Inspector.

–And now, Mr. Provincial Chief, can I bring my weapon? –Inspector Borrull asked sarcastically.

–Keep your comments inspector and get in the car!

———————

At that same moment, Estela was getting off the plane once it had landed at the Barcelona airport. She thought she had to look for help because her two stupid friends had gone to fight on their own against those murderers. She went to a telephone booth and located in the listing the number of the church where his grandmother Crisol was hiding and where all that madness began.

-Hi who is this? –Answered the priest of the church.

–Hello, good morning, could I contact Crisol Portabella, I am his granddaughter Estela!

–It's for you, it's your granddaughter!

-Dear! Thank goodness you called me, I was starting to worry about you, where are you? Are you okay?

–Yes, it's a bit long to explain, a lot of things have happened, would you come look for me at the airport!

–Sure, sure, give me a few seconds to get dressed and I'll be there right away.

–Get dressed but if it's mid-afternoon?

–Yes I know, but you don't want me to go naked to look for you.

-Then you! The man from before?... Oh, okay, okay, it doesn't matter, I'll wait for you here –said Estela nervously and hung up the phone.

"Go, go to my grandmother," she said to herself.

While waiting, sitting on a curb, she thought about how she would locate Sevange and Simon wondered if, at such a distance from the airport to the city, her feeling-desire would work to locate them as she did when during a "witch flight" they fell into a lake. In that nebulous place, in search of the Black Lady, after a few attempts something changed and she began to feel the proximity of Sevange. She got up from the curb and began to walk, guided by a sensation. She entered the terminal. She headed in the direction of some offices. which were located on one side of the lobby until finally through a window he could see Sevange with some police officers.

–Fuck Simon! We were a couple of three –Estela lamented.

In one of the police stations of the terminal guarded by police, Sevange was sitting, resting her head on the table with her hands, something she did when she wanted to clarify her ideas. Suddenly she raised her head and looked in all directions. She had noticed Estela's desire to find her.

–What's wrong! Something's wrong!

–Nothing, I just remembered something! –Sevange dissimulated.

Shortly after, Crisol arrived in a car at the door of the terminal where Estela was. When the car stopped, grandmother and granddaughter merged into a long hug.

–Grandma, I have a lot to tell you, but now we have to help Sevange, the police have detained her, it is surely Simon's work.

–I imagine why, your grandfather did the same with us, he is a man and a police officer, you know what they think, it

is a maneuver to protect you and Sevange, what are you doing dressed as a man? Well, anyway, we have to come up with a plan, let's go around the premises.

After walking around the back of the Crisol terminal he saw numerous dog cages that the police use to detect

illegal merchandise, the poor animals desperately wanted to get out of their confinement.

–Well we already have a plan, Estela, go to where Sevange is when you see the opportunity, you will get her out of there, while I will be with the car running.

In a few minutes, a horde of dogs were running excitedly through all the airport facilities. When the police saw them,

they ran after them to catch them, at which point Estela took advantage to open the door where they were holding Sevange.

–Come on baby, let's get out of here!

-Wake!! I felt like you would come looking for me.

Holding hands they began to walk quickly along the walls until they could turn the corner of the terminal.

–Thank you for coming to rescue me. Why are you wearing men's clothes? Nice hat!

At that moment the police realized that the woman they had arrested had escaped and they were running in the direction of the two of them. Sevange thought he had to act quickly, he pounced on Estela and kissed her on the mouth

in a long kiss while the police officers police passed by. Estela stood paralyzed, staring with wide eyes at Sevange.

"It's... It's the love filter," Sevange stammered.

–Yes, yes that must be it, now we are leaving, my grandmother Crisol is waiting for us with the car running.

In a matter of seconds they got into the car and hurried out of the airport.

–Good distraction strategy Crisol and thanks for helping me. What happened to the dogs? "Well, okay," Sevange said smiling.

–You're welcome, dear, in one of the cages there was a dog, so I put a few drops of the love filter on the rest, you already know the rest. Tell me Estela how you found Sevange.

–I use the love filter, I focus emotionally on Sevange and the fragrance takes me to her.

–That is not possible dear, the effect is diluted in a day, it is for single use, use a tenth of a drop of the love filter, the rest is orange blossom oil. Estela and Sevange looked at each other for a moment and then changed the direction of their eyes. Crisol drove the car along the road from the airport to the city, Estela

explained everything they had experienced because of all the dangers they had overcome, her grandmother was the aroma archive, she had the obligation to memorize the stories of witches.

–I hope it is written somewhere, this is not something you experience every day, grandma.

–Don't worry, baby, I have a secret diary, I have also experienced mine, our memories speak of what we have been as women and witches, but don't talk about this with anyone.

And now how about we go to the cemetery to look for clues like in the old days with Severina and Angélica. Do you have a weapon for me? A gun?

Estela and Sevange looked at each other, she was surprised by Crisol's attitude.

–You miss your blue-haired witch friends, don't you, Grandma.

–The truth is that yes. Those bitches left me alone.

In Crisol's memories, the images of her friends were grouped when they went to look for her or rather to rescue her from the times they lived in the United States of America, how they worked together to make magical perfumes, how one day they entered a strange fog. and they disappeared, leaving her behind.

–Lavender and Cagliostro are behind the Crimson perfume, we need to know what they did when they came to Barcelona –Sevange asked, breaking the melting pot line of thinking.

–They explained to me that when the viceroy came back from the colonies to live in the city and ordered the construction of a palace in the middle of the Ramblas de las Flores to supply herself, at that time there were many sellers of floral botany and plant oils, that way manufacturing his perfumes, he later joined the Perfumed Society in his own right where he had a prominent role for his knowledge of magical perfumes, it was also said that he had the help of a very attractive alchemist lover.

–Yes, we have met that man –Sevange confirmed.

–One day while the two were working on a mysterious fragrance in the greenhouse that was on the upper roof of the house in the shape of a skylight, a strange light appeared that came from nowhere, surrounded the mansion and they both disappeared. End of the story, dear girls .

–Which means that we do not have graves or tombstones where we can look for any sign or clue –Estela pointed out.

-Crisol, you said that Lavanda the Vicereina joined the Perfumed Society, that means that at its headquarters there will be her coat of arms, coats of arms and banners, there

we could find something that tells us where the scarf is - said Sevange.
At that moment Crusol stopped the car immediately.
–Shall we look for a big handkerchief? What happened to the Crimson Angel?
–It's a bit long to explain, the two things are the same, but I think Sevange is right, we should go to the Perfumed Society. Can you take us?
–Yes, yes of course I am the Aroma Archive!
The rest of the car ride was done in silence. Crisol looked in the rearview mirror at the faces of Estela and Sevange and thought he saw that they were no longer the same people, although it had been years since he had seen his granddaughter and Sevange even though it was his protected, she had a very different line of thought than her grandmother Severina, whom she knew very well.
–The lived experience makes you a witch and the more devastating it is, the better witch you are, that is how our
world is, sometimes very beautiful, sometimes cruel and always lonely, as well as attractive, like the best lover is what we fear, the unknown
–Crisol recited-

Well we have arrived at the perfume museum, the headquarters of the Perfumed Society is hidden in a secret gallery.
–Isn't it reckless to hide in a public place like a museum?
–No Estela! Everyone looks at it and no one sees it, that is the best hiding place for us.
Once they got out of the car they entered the museum courtyard and headed to the glassed-in booth of the guard and doorman when they entered the small room a woman came out to meet them.

-Melting pot! What are you doing here? Our teacher would not like to see you in these dangerous moments.

–I know very well Arcanum zero, but it is vitally important that we enter, there are lives in danger.

–Well, okay, if the extremely serious situation requires it, go ahead. Hello Sevange! And who is this young woman?

"She is my granddaughter, the botanical witch Estela," answered Crisol. The zero Arcanum corresponds to the Tarot card the Fool, it has the function of guarding the holy places of botanical witchcraft. The woman went to a corridor and in the corner

of the wall, she activated a spring that made a wooden panel opened and revealed a long corridor illuminated by antique lamps shaped like torches that ended in a spacious room where in its center there was a large circular table where the members of the Perfumed Society met with the teacher Nuria Gaudi at the head.

Estela was impressed seeing the shelves illuminated with thousands of perfume bottles and containers with exotic flowers from which they extract essential oils to make the best fragrances in the world.

All the members of the circular table present turned their faces to the newcomers.

-Melting pot! I hope you have a good reason to come here at times like this, our rules don't allow it.

–I have it, teacher Nuria, my granddaughter Estela, Sevange and the grandson of the witch Angelica, the policeman Simon Borrull, have made a flight to the past in search of the crimson angel by which we have been attacked and three of our sisters have been kidnapped, well. You have to know that they have faced witch hunters, inquisitors with matches in their hands, and revolutionary soldiers. Estela has a gunshot wound, they have been on the verge of being burned to death and they have returned to the present to finish the mission. To do this, Estela has escaped from a hospital and Sevange is being chased by the police. So Nuria, don't give me rules when you are

sitting here warm and doing nothing except talking about perfumes.

-Melting pot ! How dare you judge us! You have to know that we also have a plan to defend our society. Over the years we have expanded our contact with democratic foreign embassies, with large industrial corporations, religious organizations all related to us, in short it is just a matter of offering the same bone to different dogs and waiting for them to fight among themselves.

–You mean that foreign secret services are involved, have you offered the crimson angel as a weapon? Have you gone crazy? -Sevange reproached.

Estela advanced towards the table and, resting her fists on it, faced the teacher of the society.

–Very intelligent teacher, but if the bone does not appear the dogs will turn against you, "dear" –said Estela angrily.

All the members of the botanical society looked towards the teacher, who raised her arms out of boredom or impotence...

-OK! In any case, nowadays young people do not respect rules or authority, not to mention the disdain they show by

not entering our secret perfumed society...What do you want!

–We want to see the coat of arms and crests of the family lineage of the witch Lavender Lavernia –said Estela.

–The vicereine? So the police, oh of course it's from the lineage of the Black Lady, that's where the Golden Skulls

I was looking for the crimson angel as I didn't realize before. They didn't find it and they went after us and especially you three.

The teacher got up from her seat and the other botanical witches did the same. With Nuria Gaudí at the head, they walked through a corridor that led to another large rectangular room in the center of the room commanded by an open coffin full of red roses. with the name of the witches written on a ribbon, those who were members of the society throughout time. On the walls of the room hung all the shields, banners, coats of arms with drawings of perfumes, angels and witches, names of fragrances that They identify the lineages of the ancient families of the society, each of them perfectly illuminated by the light of a small lantern Estela stopped at a jar that caught her attention.

–Wow, how curious! The design of this perfume is inspired by the expiatory temple of the Sagrada Familia.

–No Estela dear! On the contrary, what you have in your hands is two millennia old. It was made in Alexandria. It belonged to Cleopatra with its fragrance. Julius Caesar and Mark Antony fell in love with her. In reality, she was not that beautiful, but she was a great botanical witch. She lived a time. difficult and he had to use poisons to survive – Crisol story.

The master of ceremonies Gaudi nodded her head as Crisol explained.

–We have arrived, there you have it.

On the vicereine's shield there was no perfume bottle drawn as was usual, instead there was the letter L repeated three times which corresponds to the name and surname, in the center a naked woman dancing with a scarf that barely covered her and which represented the twenty-first Arcanum which is the world in the tarot card that belonged to him by date of birth

and on the banner he had drawn an alabaster jar and several Goose.

Estela contemplated all this with a hypnotic gaze, an avalanche of images of everything she had experienced a few days ago: the flights, the insane asylum and vampires, the Black Lady, the viceroy's mansion, the attractive alchemist, the men fighting until they died for the dance. sensual and mortal of the vicereine. At that moment the whole puzzle was solved in his mind and a feeling of admiration overcame him towards those two witches Vangeli and Lavanda, two women who survived difficult times persecuted by inquisitors and witch hunters.

All eyes were focused on Estela, her beatified face and her smile revealed that she had discovered something important.

–The vicereine's scarf is hidden in the map of the botanical witches, which is none other than...

chapter 9
The Palace of Death

In the offices of the American consulate in Barcelona, Inspector Simon Borrull, sitting in a comfortable chair, resting his hands on a long table, tried to remain calm. He had been in that office for an hour in the company of several guys who were in no way diplomatic personnel. It seemed like they were expecting someone important and he needed a drink like never before. He had the feeling that he had been a fool for having made decisions on his own and not having stormed the vicereine's palace in the company of Sevange and Estela.

–Well, how about someone offers me something strong to drink, now thanks to you I'm not on duty. Who are we waiting for?

When the inspector finished the sentence, a middle-aged man entered the room, he was wearing an expensive suit, he had an upright bearing, the other men stood at attention

in front of him, as expected, he surely had military rank, he walked a few meters until he was in front of the inspector. I look at him with indifference.

–Mr. Borrull, I demand that you get up!!! The provincial police chief shouted.

–It doesn't matter, leave it. Mr. Garmendia, I am very grateful to you for your collaboration, now you can leave us alone and I repeat, I thank you on behalf of all the American diplomatic personnel in Spain, and I will extend my gratitude to the Minister.

The provincial police chief slammed his heel that almost broke the floor. He pressed his hands to his hips and raised his head with his chin touching the lamp in a helpful manner.

-Always at your service!! You have me at your entire disposal, gentlemen.

And immediately he left the room with a martial step. The man who had entered a few seconds ago pulled out a chair and sat down opposite Inspector Borrull.

–Mr. Inspector, my name is Ronald Maxwell and I am the security secretary of the American embassy in Madrid. You may wonder why you are here, first of all you should

know that you are not detained and that we have only invited you to this office to ask you some questions.

–I understand that the guests are offered something to drink.

–Of course, of course you would like a whiskey, a brandy, a soft drink

–A brandy!

Seconds later one of the men guarding the door approached with a tray of drinks, while the security secretary took an object out of his jacket pocket.

–Do you recognize this police badge, Mr. Inspector?

–You know very well that it is mine. By the way, where was it days ago when I lost it? - the inspector asked, feigning surprise.

–It says his name is Simon Borrull Levy, class of the year 1962, but he says that he lost it a few days ago as it is almost two hundred years old. It was unearthed in the ruins of a military fort in New Orleans.

The inspector was in a bind, there was no sensible explanation that was credible for this contradiction. He

remembered that in some newsstands there were some new publications that talked about flying saucers and extraterrestrial visits that had numerous followers.

–Well, I think I'll have to tell it even at the risk of being expelled from the police for being crazy.

I was kidnapped by Martians who took me to their ship through a beam of light. The next thing I remember is that I woke up in another country in a place full of swamps and in a past time.

–You are kidding me, I do not advise you to do it, Mr. Borrull.

–Then how do you explain that my police badge is two hundred years old, Mr. Maxwell, you don't believe that I have a time machine. It's clearly a fake!

The security secretary leaned back in his chair, ran his hand over his chin, and finally stood up and approached his men. They spoke quietly and in English for a short time.

–Well, let's move on to something else, who knows about an international mafia organization that is operating in Barcelona.

Inspector Simon Borrull had realized that those guys were disoriented and were acting blindly; they did not have

accurate information about what was happening. He thought that he should provide information that they already possessed in order to get out of the interrogation well.

–A few days ago I went to the island of Ibiza following a lead and there I was attacked by some guys who apparently had many resources

I was able to narrow down one of them, he told me that they were members of a sect called "Golden Skulls" and that they were looking for a perfume called Crimson Angel.

–Yes, if we know all that, we have an infiltrator in that organization, we believe that the perfume is a code name for a device to travel to the past.

–Ha, ha, ha and you think that I have that device, that's why they brought me here! Hours ago we had to rescue some young girls that those thugs have kidnapped and you have ruined the operation because you think I have a toy to go to the past. You have gone crazy! –The inspector shouted angrily.

–Don't be angry, we have authorization to keep you here as long as necessary and by the way, that order, the "Golden Skulls" ceased to exist at the same time and place that your police badge was buried.

–How? Isn't it an order of religious fanatics?

–They belong to one of the most powerful mafia families in America, the Gambinos.

Tell me where the rescue operation was going to be carried out, it is possible that the bosses are there and we can stop them.

–In the Vicereina palace on Las Ramblas in Barcelona, I am going with you.

–No, Mr. Inspector, this is an internal matter, you will stay here as our guest for the moment, make yourself comfortable, the bar cabinet is open.

"It means forced guest," replied the inspector, looking at the bouncers guarding the door.

They all left the room, leaving only Inspector Simón Borrull sitting with the only company of some glasses and some bottles of brandy. He got up to pour himself a drink, but he put the bottle back in its place. He thought it wouldn't be fair to raise his elbow while Some girls kidnapped by the mafia are in danger, the men who had invited him to the consulate were carrying weapons if they attack the Vicereina's palace, the night could end in a bloodbath.

After an hour the doorbell rang and one of the men who was watching the inspector went to the front door.

"Good evening, I'm Agent Albert Cusidó. I've come to bring a message from Provincial Chief Garmendia to Inspector

Borrull," the agent told him while showing him his credentials.

–Give me the message and I will send it to you.

"Okay, here it is," he said while pointing his gun at him.

Agent Cusido along with several police officers freed Inspector Borrull, the two consulate guards were put in handcuffs tied to one of the legs of the solid table in the room, at which time the inspector was able to recover his pistol.

–Thank you Albert, let's go before it's too late.

-Mister! I have a patrol car on the corner. By the way, the woman detained at the airport has escaped. Do you want me to issue a search warrant?

–No, no, it's better this way. And the woman admitted to the hospital in Ibiza?

–Same sir, he also fled.

"Well, let's go," the inspector smiled.

They quickly got into the car, accompanied by two more police officers from the unit. Once driving, the police inspector thought he smelled several perfumes in addition to his own, but that didn't matter now, he had to arrive as soon as possible, the night had fallen upon them and I feared the worst, in fifteen minutes they arrived at the Vicereina's palace, they got out of the car, they saw several cars with official license plates clearly indicating that they were inside but there was no one at the entrance door of the Vicereina's palace,

there was no agent from the consulate Everything about the embassy wasn't very strange either.

"Sir, the door is open," said Agent Cusido, surprised.

It is known to everyone that a situation is dangerous when it begins with an open door. At that moment they all took out their pistol and gently pushed the enormous entrance gate. They walked through the interior patio where they entered the building.

After passing the old horse-driven carriages, darkness covered the entire place. Luckily, they saw several lanterns lit on the ground that they picked up.

"My God, this place is full of corpses," said one of the police officers, scared.

"There has been a massacre here, the blood runs down the steps, the floor is full of bullet casings, it would seem that all of them have emptied their magazines," police agent Cusido commented in astonishment.

An icy cold ran through the inspector's spine, from the base to the nape of his neck. He had had the pleasure of knowing about this type of death and he did not like it at all. He felt that they were going to face the unknown.

–None of these men have gunshot wounds, their bodies are torn and devoured, there is an expression of terror on their faces.

–Sir, it means that they have shot in all directions because they have panicked.

–I want you to get out of here, it is very dangerous that...

He did not finish the sentence when shouts for help were heard coming from the upper rooms. They ran up the side stairs and climbed onto a landing. They stumbled upon more dead people in the darkness. This time it was the American staff of the consulate, one of them was Ronald Maxwell. secret agent of the American embassy killed in

the same circumstances shone the flashlights on their faces and had the same expression of fear and pain.

–This is where the cries for help came from.

One of the policemen went ahead to say while he was running down a hallway when he pushed open the door, a horde of horrible putrid specters fell on him as if he were a meal that they had to devour with a lust for life to absorb the life force of the body, at the same time. while the police officer screamed in pure terror.

–They are killing Francisco! – Agent Cusido shouted as he ran firing his gun to save his partner.

–Nooo, damn Albert is back!!! Carlos give me that decorative Torch on the wall, wrap it with that piece of curtain and now light it while I spray it with the brandy from the flask, stand behind me

–Albert, Albert answer! The inspector shouted as he waved the torch on both sides of his body to make his way through those horrible creatures with emaciated bodies that were devouring the wounded agent.

–The fire makes them retreat. Lord, they are living dead!!! – Agent Carlos shouted scared, when he focused his flashlight on them.

Fear took hold of him and he ran down the stairs with the misfortune that he stumbled in the darkness with the bodies of the dead gangsters falling to the ground and his hope of getting out of there alive vanished, it only took a

few seconds for his screams to echo. through the walls of the palace of death and then silence.

Inspector Simon Borrull had been left alone, waving the torch to ward off the horrible creatures around him, when only a few meters away he could see a glass vault with a door in the center and near it he saw something that squeezed the bodies in his stomach. of his police friends Albert and Francisco.

When suddenly he heard a voice as if it came from the bottom of a cave.

–You are the foreigner, witness of my cruel destiny. Where is the Vicereina?

The inspector turned his head and saw the figure of a being appear in the darkness with a deformed body burned and his face completely disfigured, and yet he had to convince himself that there had to be a face there.

–I am the inquisitor of New Spain, and at his side Captain Avellaneda recognized him by his uniform. The witch Vicereine took over our will and our souls, we want her to grant us rest in eternity.

At that moment, Inspector Simón Borrull's images of those terrible moments returned to his mind and also the face of Monsignor Fray Mateo de Azuaga.

"The vicereine does not exist, it has been one hundred and eighty years since you all died," Inspector Simon argued.

–You don't understand, we cannot die, we are condemned to a curse that forces us to kill and devour human life.

The inspector remembered the words of Lavender Lavernia "fight until you die for your mistress, the witch vicereine of New Orleans."

"Only she can break the curse of the crimson angel," the inspector recited in a low voice.

With his hand back, Inspector Simon turned the knob of the greenhouse door and closed it behind him. He thought he was safe for the moment. He remembered that witches always have a secret exit, but he didn't have time to look for it. The horrendous creatures were pressing the door with such force that the glass frames were going to break into pieces at any moment, the strange thing is that there were perfumes and cultivated plants perfectly cataloged, the greenhouse was used by someone.

In a corner were the kidnapped girls tied hand and foot. The inspector took a sharp spatula to remove the dirt and cut the ties.

–Don't worry, I'm a police officer and I'm going to get you out of here.

–Sir, they kidnapped us, they wanted us to make a very strange perfume. What are those monsters? –one of the girls asked scared.

–I wouldn't know how to explain it! But now the important thing is to save life.

He tried to open a small window in the glass roof of the greenhouse that would give him access to the roof of the palace and save the lives of all of them, but it was stuck, the latch was rusty, he tried hard, he only managed to scratch his hand, the door began to break the glass. They fell to the ground one after another. He took out his gun and shot the window bolt, which flew into the air.

–Get on this chair and go out through this skylight, we will escape through the roof.

One after another they managed to reach the roof of the vicereine's palace and escape at least for the moment. When the inspector tried to climb out of the window, one of the emaciated ghosts jumped on top of him and bit him between the base of his neck and shoulder, causing a cataract of blood while screaming in pain, Inspector Simon grabbed a hook-shaped tool and stuck it in his head, falling to the ground writhing in spasms, he had no time to waste, he grabbed the window frame and with his hands he pushed himself up and He was able to get outside at the same time that the murderous ghosts entered, destroying the cabin, and shortly after their burned bodies broke through the glass of the greenhouse roof and crawled dangerously close to them.

"The pilot light above the greenhouse door frame prevented them from entering," one of the girls shouted.

The inspector observed that in a corner of the palace where they were there was a streetlight on. He pointed his gun at the glass to gain more light and fired. For the moment they were safe.

chapter 10

The thirteen geese

-The goose game! –Sevange confirmed.

–Exactly! We have to leave quickly –Estela hastened to say, addressing Crisol and Sevange.

-Wait! What will you do when you find the Crimson Angel? –asked Nuria Gaudi.

"Destroy it," said Sevange.

–Today is the time, Saint John's Day, witches' night –Crisol stated.

The perfumed society teacher nodded her head and sighed in relief. Once on Calle Sevange and Crisol stopped in front of Estela.

–Well, where is the perfume? Crisol asked.

–Actually the Black Lady gave us clues at all times about where the crimson angel would be in the future, which is

today, she always helped us and saved my life, what a woman! –said Estela with admiration.

–It's strange, the woman I knew was a ruthless witch and knowing that you would go to meet her on a flight to the past filled me with panic, I have to confess –Crisol admitted.

–I believe that Vangeli felt affection towards her, that's why she protected you from that soldier and lost her borrowed life –Sevange said.

–Yes, I think that's how it happened. The night we were in the viceroy's mansion we entered the vicereine's room while the alchemist was sleeping, after writing on the foular the magical formulas of the lucis spell with the perfume of the crimson angel, Lavender met with the Black Lady and there was where they devised the plan, so that two hundred years later it would be found by us and we could defend ourselves from our enemies.

–And you say that those clues are hidden in the witches' map, (the goose game) –asked Sevange.

–Yes, the flights we made from one place to another are the squares of the Goose game.

–From Goose to Goose –Sevange confirmed.

–At the beginning we flew to the insane asylum and vampires, (the Prison) –said Estela.

–And from there to the lake that is (the Well) of sadness, –completed Sevange.

– Which took us to the Black Lady's mansion –

(the Inn) – Estela continued.

–Later we arrived in New Orleans crossing a bridge and we left it through another bridge that we destroyed. Do you remember that?

–From bridge to bridge –Sevange confirmed.

–That a short time later he took us to the viceroy's palace where the Beast (Labyrinth) was located in the basement.

"That was where the black lady saved Estela's life," Sevange recalled.

–Yes, and that is why he randomly found –Death– which in the game box is number fifty-eight, the two numbers add up to thirteen which is the number of Geese in the game –Estela continued.

–Of course the thirteen Geese of Saint Eulalia that are in the Barcelona cathedral! There is the Vicereine's Foulard –Sevange responded.

Saint Eulalia was a shepherd girl from Goose who lived in Barcelona in the 3rd century AD. She was executed by order of the Roman Emperor Diocletian for refusing to renounce her Christian faith. She was thirteen years old. In her honor there are thirteen geese in the cloister of the cathedral. from Barcelona.

–And I return to the starting square, were the last words of the black lady –Estela remembered sadly.

–Let's go girls! Let's go to the Cathedral, I'll call Father Herminio so he can open the cloister door for us and get us a map of witches, ahh

I wanted something like that, you really don't have a weapon for me? Crisol asked.

–We don't have weapons, grandma, but Sevange is enough for us.

–I hope I don't have to fight with the Geese –they all laughed.

They walked with an urgent step, they were determined to find the foular and put an end to all that, after walking several streets they arrived at the side of the Barcelona Cathedral and after passing under the skull bridge they arrived at where the entrance to the cloister was, they called the porch knocking with the knocker.

–Welcome to the present, I am Father Herminio.

Estela and Sevange looked at Crisol in surprise.

"Well, we both share fragrances," Crisol responded, touching the hair that covered his neck.

–Well, we're inside, now we have to look for clues. Do you have the map of the botanical witches? –Estela concluded.

"Yes, the Goose game, here it is," Father Herminio handed him.

–We start the game with the entrance to the cloister from square one – explained Sevange.

–Now we walk through this gallery until we reach one of the tombs that is on the ground and that is the one of the innkeepers guild "la posada" – Estela argument.

–Well, let's continue this way, and turning the corner along this corridor we arrive at the tomb of the master builders of the "water well" – Sevange discovered.

–Like in the old days – Crisol shouted excitedly.

–Now we have to look for the "Labyrinth" – said Sevange.–that strange, according to the Goose game, it had to be here, although it is possible that this time we will have to look at the walls.

–For example this door. "Which is from the chapel of the burned witches, carved like a hieroglyph or labyrinth with a lion's head in the center," Crisol pointed out proudly.

They opened the door to enter but they stepped back with their arms raised several armed men pointed at their heads, those men were well dressed in elegant black suits with faces seasoned in doing a lot of harm to people and behind them an old man leaning on a cane that walked with difficulty but maintained a bearing of authority that showed that he was the leader of the group of criminals that had them surrounded.

–Hello Crisol, how long has it been since we saw each other? Thirty, forty years? and yet your face does not reflect the passage of time.

–Lucas Sorni!! You are the one behind all this. How? -she said stunned.

–Now my name is Joe Gambino and I have another family in America, although I have always remembered the time we lived together in this city, and this is Estela, our granddaughter, right? I know everything about you. But let's get to the matter at hand.

I have stayed alive thanks to some clinics in Switzerland and their health programs in addition to the complete blood

change, but the body can't handle it anymore and I need something more powerful.

I have searched for Severina and Angelica all over the world, they had the perfume of the eternal youth of the angel Luzbel and I wanted to have that power but I was not successful, despite how much is said about them I never found them, and my time was spent. It ends as you can see, but a few weeks ago I received information about a perfume of ancient power from witches and alchemists, so reviewing your history of witchcraft, we posed as the Golden Skulls, your ancient enemies.

"To get us to the surface," Sevange concluded.

–Sometimes you have to insert a stick into the burrow to make the rabbit come out.

–How have you changed, Lucas? When I met you, you had the charm of naivety.

–Time takes everything Crisol and gives nothing back. I recognize that you women of your lineage have something that makes you special, in some way you always preserve that mysterious halo that the passage of time cannot erase.

–Remember that Adam lost paradise for biting Eve's apple and that the Angels fell from heaven for looking at us so much, so we women have something, right? –Crisol threatened.

–Surely so, now dear, give me the Vicereina's scarf.

"The crimson Angel perfume that is written on it is very dangerous, Grandpa," Estela said worriedly.

–I have nothing to lose, dear granddaughter.

–Lucas you are not going to shoot your family! Crisol shouted.

-You're right!

The mobster made a gesture to one of his men who shot Father Herminio who fell backwards to the ground with a wound in his chest.

–Lucaaas!! Damn you Bastard! Crisol shouted.

"And the next one will be Sevange," he threatened, pointing the gun of one of his men at his head.

"Okay, okay, okay, I'll find the scarf and you can go to hell with it," Estela shouted.

"If someone tries to play this trick with me, you won't get out of here alive," Lucas Sorni threatened.

The mafia boss ordered his men to follow Estela and Sevange on their tour of the Cloister, while Crisol tried to revive the injured priest without success.

– Well, let's continue according to the map we must look for the Jail box

They advanced a few meters looking for clues on the floor, walls and windows, something related to a prison. Estela and Sevange scrutinized everything they found.

Surrounding them at that moment, the priest who was badly injured on the floor pointed to the vaulted ceiling, where there was a relief in the shape of a medallion on which he had sculpted the martyred prisoners imprisoned in remote times. Estela and Sevange followed the dying priest's instructions with their gaze. ,

–We have the "Prison", now according to the map we have to continue through this other gallery –Estela hastened to say.

–Well, where is he?–the mafia boss was impatient.

–We are missing the final square, which according to the game, is in the Goose yard –Sevange concluded.

"The foular scares me so much, like these murderous guys, I'm scared shitless," Estela hurriedly said in Sevange's ear.

–What is the final box? –asked Lucas Sorni.

-Death! -Sevange said defiantly.

In the central part of the cloister was the Patio de las Ocas surrounded by three-meter-high bars with a metal door that gave access to the interior where there was a stone fountain and a small pond where the animals swam.

They pushed the door but it did not open, it was closed with a padlock, Lucas Sorni made a gesture with his head and one of his men shot the bolt which flew into the air causing a circular echo that reverberated throughout the premises.

The Geese began to flutter scared, they all joined together in a corner of the garden behind some palm trees. Once inside...

–Don't make noise! These animals are territorial and will attack us if they feel threatened – explained Sevange.

–What are we looking for? –asked Lucas Sorni aka Joe Gambino.

–A symbol that has to do with death or perhaps with the final arcana the World, with a naked woman –Estela explained.

They searched among the weeds for the walls of the fountain, the sides of the pond in the small animal house, Estela looked at the witches map again and this time she raised it above her head and drew a straight line from the roof where little before they saw the symbol of the imprisoned martyrs up to the box

death and with surprise he saw that he marked the corner where the Geese were grouped.

–It's there Sevange! -The two friends looked at each other with fear.

–It seems that they are guarding the Foular –said Estela with a soft voice.

The head of the mafia group along with his men advanced, scaring away the animals that ran and hid behind the pond, revealing a slab on the wall.

–There is a drawing of a naked dancing woman engraved in the relief on the wall –Estela explained.

–We have found it, very good dear granddaughter, now hand it over to me.

Estela hesitantly remembered the terrible scenes she witnessed on her Flight to the past.

-I will do it! Crucible said glaring at the man who was once her boyfriend in the past.

He had entered the central patio seconds before, when his dear friend Father Herminio left the world of the living.

He pressed the slab, rotating the relief of the woman's drawing, and it easily opened, revealing a leather saddlebag.

-Here you have it! I hope you live many years to remember your crimes. Lucas Sorni finally had in his hands the object that he had wanted so much, something that would allow him to regenerate his body and extend his life.

– – – – –

At that moment, on the other side of the city on the roof of the palace of death, Inspector Simón Borrull and the kidnapped perfumer girls were trying to save their lives.

"Let's go to this corner, it's brighter, we'll be safe here," Inspector Borrull said without much conviction.

"The dead keep advancing towards us," one of the girls shouted in fear.

–On that ledge there is an external rain drain pipe, you can go down there, while I will stop you with the gun.

Simon knew he couldn't stop those monsters, but there were already too many dead for tonight and the only honorable action left was to save the lives of those girls.

Suddenly police sirens were heard surrounding the vicereine's palace.

–Now try to get down quickly!

While they went down the drain pipe and saved their lives, the inspector faced, gun in hand, these creatures condemned not to die.

"Well, this is the end, if I have to die, let it be as a botanical witch and a perfumed policeman," he said to himself.

He took from his pocket the perfume of his Arcanum by birth the Moon, the tarot card of integrated duality (now in those final moments of his life

everything made sense to him) he spread the fragrance throughout his body at the same time he raised his weapon and pointed it at the horrible creatures.

but suddenly something happened, the living dead that had Inspector Simon Borrull surrounded stopped.

–I feel the power of the vicereine witch of New Orleans! –The voice of the dead inquisitor was heard and in a few seconds they disappeared across the roof.

Simon guessed that this meant that Estela and Sevange had found the damn foular and were therefore in danger.

He entered the greenhouse again and left from there down the stairs to the interior patio where the chief commissioner was accompanied by agents from his unit looking surprised at the number of corpses scattered there.

–Borrull! For heaven's sake, what happened here? You are injured, we have an ambulance on the street.

–Mr. Commissioner, I have lost my men in the rescue of the women perfumers, tomorrow I will present the report to you.

–Do not blame yourself for what happened, the idiot provincial chief Garmendia is responsible for delaying the rescue operation for hours, perhaps this massacre would

have been avoided. I will give part of it to the Ministry of the Interior.

While they were talking, several sirens of police cars could be heard driving in another direction.

who were there, Inspector Simón looked at the commissioner with surprise.

–We have received a call reporting the entry of some armed men into the cathedral –explained the commissioner.

–With your permission, sir, I'm taking this police motorcycle, I'm going to the cathedral to finish this story.

"You go, and remember it's not your fault," the commissioner shouted as the inspector rode away on the motorcycle.

"Besides, now all the police wear perfume," he expressed regretfully to himself.

With his shirt torn and stained with blood, wanting to vomit, disgusted, angry with everyone and with himself for having lost his men, his few friends that he had, Albert, Francisco, Carlos now dead, he had saved the captive girls but This did not make him feel any less guilty because the men he their position they did not know what they were facing, because they had been stupid to believe that the damned handkerchief would be hidden in the Vicereina's palace, no woman would hide something so dangerous in her house, her

home and, most importantly, the matters that begin with Botanical witchcraft ends in the same way, even the stupidest knows that, he shouldn't have left Estela and Sevange out of it - Inspector Simon thought while driving the motorcycle,

— — — — — —

In the cathedral of Barcelona the situation was no better than that experienced minutes before in the vicereine's palace.

Lucas Sorni examined the saddlebag and concluded that it was about two hundred years old. He nervously took off his jacket and shirt, leaving his torso bare, lifted the zipper and removed the scarf that with the contact of his skin took on a life of its own and surrounded his body.

"Yes, now I feel its power, I want to be young again, for my body to regain its youth, its childish vitality," he shouted and laughed, while his eyes turned red like flames of fire.

The dark clear and starry sky changed to a sinister crimson color that covered the entire courtyard of the Cloister, the Geese screamed in fright, the visual and acoustic scene that echoed through the walls was horrendous.

"Let's get out of here quickly," Sevange ordered fearfully.

They ran towards the door to escape but the mafia boss's men pointed their guns at them, preventing them from leaving center field.

Estela, Sevange and Crisol were trapped but something made those thugs retreat with a terrified expression.

The floor and walls of the cloister were covered with funerary tombstones of nobles and great people from the medieval era and the Renaissance of the city of Barcelona, an entry route for the dead condemned by a curse in New Orleans long ago. The ghostly specters came out of the tombs, pounced on them, and they fired their weapons in all directions.

It was of no use, the place was filled with screams of pain and panic.

–Get on the ground or we will die. What are those horrible burnt specters? -Crisol shout.

At that moment Simon Borrull entered the scene pushing the interior door of the cathedral that gave access to the cloister. He lit a flare that he was carrying on the motorcycle and ran to meet Estela, Sevange and Crisol.

–This way, witches!

–Simon!! We follow you – Estela shouted when she saw him.

They ran and arrived at the wake of the chapel of the burned witches, a metal shelf where the candles that luckily were lit are placed.

The cursed undead had them surrounded but they could not pass through the light that way they were safe.

–Simon! Those ghostly beings are what I think they are.

–Yes Sevange, the soldiers, inquisitors and witch hunters who died in a horrible way in the palace of the Viceroy of New

Orleans, are possessed by the curse of the crimson angel. We have to destroy the vicereine's scarf.

Inside the patio Lucas Sorni was shouting euphorically, oblivious to everything that was happening around him.

–I have defeated time, I am getting younger –he laughed hysterically.

But the process did not stop and the transformation continued more and more, until her clothes covered her small naked body.

–No, no, stop! stop this! I don't want to be a child, noooooo...

In a few minutes the body of Lucas Sorni became that of a three-year-old boy who was then attacked by the thirteen

Geese until his horrible screams could no longer be heard along with those of his hitmen, silence and blood in the sand of the lower cloister. a reddish-crimson sky.

–Sevange returns! Damn!

Inspector Simon shouted. Sevange was the Strength, in the Arcanum of the Tarot his mission was to protect them all and that was what he was going to do, he ran towards the fence attached to a half wall that surrounded the Goose patio and with a jump typical of an Olympic athlete he was able to Entering and approaching the dead man-child, he picked up the scarf from the ground and raised it above his head at which point the horrible march of condemned undead stopped.

–Leave now! "I won't be able to hold them for long!" Sevange shouted.

–We're not going to leave, I'm the crazy one here! –Estela responded that she was preparing to meet her.

Simon stopped her by grabbing her arm.

–Wait, take this flare, I will go with Sevange, the dead cannot stand the light, I will throw the scarf at you and when you have it, light the flare and run until you leave the cathedral, there is a bonfire in the middle of the square,

tonight is the night of Saint John, you already know what you have to do.

"Please get out of here, I won't be able to hold on much longer," Sevange begged.

Simon tore off a piece of the splintered door, which as fate would have it was called the Chapel of the Burning Witches, took off his bloody shirt and made himself a torch.

–Wait, Simon, with this essential oil the fire will last longer – Crisol explained.

He advanced down the hallway of the cloister with the lit torch, causing the ghostly horde of undead to retreat until they reached the courtyard where Sevange was.

–The fire will protect us, don't worry, now put the crimson angel in the saddlebag and throw it to Estela.

–Are you sure Simon?

-Now!

Sevange threw it in the direction where Estela was, which she picked up in the air with a jump. She lit the flare and

they left the wake, running together with Crisol towards the main exit from the cloister, pursued by those condemned not to die. When they arrived, the door did not open until it seemed to be blocked.

- Fuck! Now I remember that the door opens by an electric mechanism, Estela, you can go through this opening, leave me the flare and destroy the damn perfume.

–I hope that my yoga sessions allow me to bend my body.

Estela tried to hold her breath and reduce her stomach until she could overcome the opening of the main door of the cathedral.

–Grandma now you! Try it, I'll help you get out.

–Dear, that is not possible, my body has its limitations. Run to the bonfire and destroy the Crimson Angel, this flare will soon go out.

Estela approached the large mass of stacked wood lit among fireworks and people who were dancing and celebrating the festival of San Juan a few meters away from where she was. He took the Vicereine's Foulard from his saddlebag and threw it at the straw doll that was at the top of the bonfire, burning the crimson angel written on the foular.

In the cloister of the cathedral, Sevange and Simón, holding hands, tried to leave the courtyard of the geese surrounded by the cursed dead of New Orleans.

"I hope Estela has made it, this is getting very ugly," Simón said while shaking the torch.

Suddenly the clouds that covered the dark sky cleared and the ghosts were expelled by an unknown force that sent them flying to the bonfire lit in the square, where the crimson angel scarf was burning.

everything was over and the curse had come to an end.

Sevange and Simon approached where Estela was contemplating the horrendous scene, as the cursed disembodied specters melted into the fire.

as the flaming straw doll lit up in a sinister orange-black color.

–Girls you have done it! –Crisol said surprised.

–Yes, grandmother, but it has been horrible. I'm not used to days like this. And you, Simón, how was your day? I see that you have a bad wound, you have to go to a hospital.

–There are wounds that a hospital cannot cure. "I have lost my Sevange men, I have led them into a death trap, Albert was only twenty-two years old," he expressed sadly as he watched the bonfire burn.

–Now I have understood the meaning of the phrase that came to our aid in difficult times –Estela commented, trying to encourage Simon.

–Forget, dream, everything begins again –Estela recited.

–You Simon are the one who forgets, Estela the one who dreams and I the one who starts again.

At that moment a sudden fog appeared at the end of the square where mysterious silhouettes of two women with blue hair appeared.

–Well dears, the time has come to meet with my friends Severina and Angelica – Crisol expressed with joy.

–Are you leaving Grandma? Where are you going!

-Who knows! The perfume of the Nolasca witch creates a fog that takes you to unknown places out of this world, it is a very ancient and mysterious fragrance.

"I need a new look at my life, Estela," he told his granddaughter while caressing her face.

–When Angelica and Severina, the blue-haired witches, left, I stayed to instruct you in this mission and only heaven knows what I had to wait for as soon as you were born, now that everything is over they have come to look for me. "Well, I hope there are men and drinks in there," she said to herself as she walked away. When she was about to enter the thickness of the fog, she stopped and turned her head.

–Sevange! –Crisol said, extending his hand.

Simon and Estela looked at each other surprised.

–When we flew to the insane asylum and vampires it was not due to Estela's imagination. It was one of my dreams, my grandmother Severina was an expert witch dreamer and she taught me that knowledge, and now she needs me. I'm sorry to have to leave, I liked it our witch triangle – explained Sevange looking at the ground sadly.

–But that is impossible! You can't fly into a dream with your physical body! Damn! –Simon shouted frustrated.

"With Estela everything is possible," Sevange smiled, looking at her.

–Now I understand your fear and sadness when we flew and fell into the fog-covered lake. you had been there before right! You are a lucid dreaming witch! –Estela

concluded and Sevange confirmed with a shake of his head while meeting with Crisol.

–You have done very well, now you know what witches do to enter the unknown. Survive! – Crisol said and then they disappeared along with the fog.

Simon and Estela stared into the distance without knowing what to say. Where? because? they asked themselves

After a few minutes of silence.

–I need someone to take me home and give me something strong to drink. I'm very tired.

–Sure, Simon, let's go to my family's house, there I'll heal your wound and we'll drink a bottle of whatever... Oh, did you know that the love filter... –Estela didn't finish talking.

-Yeah? What happens with it.

"Nothing, nothing, we are a couple of three," Estela stated, looking back.

–Yes, we will wait for Sevange wherever he went – Simon said cheerfully.

As they walked away through the city.

end